SAM CHEEVER

Electric Prose Publications

Mucky Bumpkin

Published by Sam Cheever
Copyright 2019 Sam Cheever

PRAISE FOR SAM CHEEVER

She might be a country girl who loves short shorts and flip-flops, but her life is less defined by her countrified attire, and more by the way she hunts down a deadly killer.

Murder is sinking its hooks into the quiet countryside and dredging up ugly secrets. *Deer Hollow* is still a quiet little town steeped in Americana and known for its delicious country fare. But being named a top ten place to live just might have inspired an assassin to make the quaint country spot home.

As Joey searches for a killer, her past is dragged from the murky darkness where she's hidden it. And secrets she never wanted to discover are rising like the stink of manure on a freshly fertilized field.

CHAPTER ONE

I've always been perfectly aware of my shortcomings as a person.

Mostly.

I consider myself generally a good person. With good instincts about people and a desire to be kind to others unless they're unkind to me. But I do have an aversion to pushy people. Which has put me on the wrong side of salesmen of all kinds more than once.

My second least favorite of these is real estate agents. Not that being a Realtor is innately bad. It's just that the act of buying or selling a house is way too much like dealing with used car salesmen for my taste.

Which brings me to my first least favorite type of salesmen.

Fortunately, it wasn't a car salesman standing on my porch that sunny, cool-ish fall day in the rural area just outside of *Deer Hollow*, *Indiana*.

But it might as well have been.

The woman standing in front of Caphy and me had lipstick on her teeth and hair that looked as if squirrels might have built it on her head for nesting. Lucky for her my dog was much more tolerant than I was. Even when she was being none-too-subtly dissed by said lipstick-teethed intruder.

"Miss Fulle, you should chain that beast up."

The hand on Caphy's collar tightened briefly as I fought to contain my instant rage. Cacophony, Caphy for short, was about the sweetest animal that ever lived. She was more than my best friend. I credited her with saving my life when I'd gone into the deepest depression imaginable after my parents were killed in a plane crash on our property.

She was also a pit bull.

And that was all some people saw when they looked at her.

Caphy smiled at the woman, her muscular tail whipping painfully against my leg. She whined softly, quivering with friendly excitement.

I drew myself up to my full five feet four inches, tucked a strand of shoulder-length red-blonde hair behind one ear, and narrowed my blue eyes at her. "She's fine," I told the woman with the squirrel's nest for hair. "She lives here. Whereas you..." I let my statement trail away, allowing my uninvited guest to gather my implication all by herself.

The woman frowned slightly, moving a purse the size of her extra-large backside in front of her like a shield. "Oh... um...okay. Well." She extended her hand a few inches in front of her, a white rectangle stuck between two short fingers. "Here's my card. My name is Penney Sellers. I was wondering if you're interested in selling your house."

I blinked several times. "Not in the least."

As I responded, I realized it was true. After my parents' death, when I initially learned that I'd inherited the house and the family auction business, my first thought was to sell the too-big house rather than live here. Too many painful memories existed within its familiar walls. I still thought I'd sell eventually. But I wasn't quite ready to make that decision.

The auction business was another matter entirely. I still hadn't accepted the responsibility they'd left in my less-than-capable hands. There was no way I could fill their shoes in the business, and being there was just too painful for me to face.

I glanced down at the card, grimacing at the obviousness of the woman's name. "Is Penney Sellers *really* your name?"

In response she gave me a slightly snotty smile. "I can offer you a premium price. There aren't many homes in this area of this quality."

"Not interested. You do know there's a huge subdivision going up on the south side of *Deer Hollow*, right?" Of course she knew that. But I was making a point.

"Those houses are fine. But they don't have the..." She swung her arms toward the pond and the trees. "Ambiance. The setting here is truly spectacular."

"Thank you. But I'm not interested in selling." I backed into the house, tugging gently on Caphy's collar. Her gaze locked onto the other woman, who'd taken a step toward the door as if she was thinking about pushing her way inside. A low growl emerged from Caphy's throat and the hair in front of her tail spiked.

Penney Sellers stopped dead in her tracks, her gaze shooting to the endlessly sweet creature who was giving her fair warning.

But Caphy's warning didn't stop the realtor's mouth from moving. "Do you own all those woods over there?" The woman asked. Her expression was perfectly innocent. But there was a gleam in her eye that I didn't like.

"Yes. All the way to the big stone marker on *Goat's Hollow Road*. 100 acres."

The gleam flared, making her look positively demonic. "A

hundred acres! My goodness. I'd love to talk to you about subdividing the property. We could build a dozen homes and still have sizeable properties."

"Not interested. Thanks for stopping by."

"But..."

I slammed the door in her face and locked it. Pressing my ear against the warm wood, I listened for her to climb into her car and drive away before I took a full breath. A soft whine drew my gaze to Caphy. "It's all right, girl. She's gone."

The pibl's tail snapped sideways once and then she nuzzled me, snorting softly. She was sensitive to my moods, and the alarm I was feeling was no doubt putting her on edge. I couldn't have explained the panic tightening my chest if someone offered me a thousand dollars to do it.

It was an unreasonable fear. But undeniable.

Nobody could force me to sell my house. Nobody could make me give up my private little wonderland. It was all I had left of my parents.

It was also the place where Caphy and I had grown up. Where we'd run and played, where I'd climbed trees and learned to swim. But the new subdivision was affecting my life in ways I hadn't expected. When I'd first learned it was coming it had seemed harmless. After all, the three hundred acre plot on the south side of *Deer Hollow* was miles away from me. The homes were supposed to be decent ones, built on quarter acre lots and not all exactly the same. I reasoned it would be nice to have some new blood in town.

Unfortunately, I hadn't counted on the other stuff that came with those homes. The constant traffic through town from looky-loos. The noise, mess, and invasion of people who thought the town had been conjured up for their enjoyment.

And the realtors, builders and construction people who clogged the streets and turned the few restaurants *Deer*

Hollow boasted into hotbeds of noise and inaccessibility at meal times.

Still, I could deal with all that.

It was the other thing that had my nerves thrumming like a banjo in the mountains of Kentucky.

The sense of impending doom.

I couldn't explain it. Hadn't experienced it before. And I suspected it had something to do with the body we'd discovered in my woods not all that long ago. I was pretty sure I wasn't completely over finding that mangled corpse or the terrifying events that came after.

Whatever the cause, it was all too real.

And it was making me as jumpy as a fat-legged frog in a French restaurant.

When the article declaring *Deer Hollow* as one of the best places to raise a family in the United States came out in the *The Indianapolis Star* weeks earlier, I'd never expected such a vast and immediate change in my world.

But suddenly the *Hollow* was on the news almost every night. Articles were being written about what a great spot it was. The local artists, authors, and businesses were being examined, highlighted, and, in some cases, given an anal probe, the likes of which the people in my little community had never experienced.

Our recent murder-driven scandal had been examined, the article's author lamenting the fact that it had apparently been overlooked when choosing America's favorite spots to live.

But, so far, my family's involvement had been blissfully absent from speculation. A fact I thought had much to do with a certain uber-sexy PI and his connections with the FBI.

For that, I was both grateful and tense.

I felt as if the other shoe was going to drop at any moment.

Two hours later, I was searching through a pile of laundry for the mate to one of my favorite socks when Hal Amity's familiar ringtone, *I'm too sexy for my shirt*, sang from the kitchen.

Caphy started bouncing around in expectation of his voice on the other end of the phone.

She had it bad.

Good thing I was a much cooler customer where Mr. Amity was involved. I grabbed my cell off the counter and hit *Answer*. "Hey, handsome. Long time no talk."

A brief silence preceded his response, delivered in his trademark smoky voice. "I called yesterday."

"Oh. Well, it seems like it's been a long time." So much for playing it cool.

Caphy barked, her nails clicking on the kitchen floor as she bounced around me, tongue lolling.

"Is that my favorite girl?"

Caphy barked again, trying to bite at the phone as she made excited, happy noises.

"She's making a fool of herself," I told him with a grin. "I really need to have the conversation with her about playing hard to get."

"And you think you're the right person for that job?" He asked. I could hear the grin in his voice.

"Hey!"

He chuckled. "Put me on speaker. I need to tell her something."

I rolled my eyes but did as he asked. "You're on."

"Hello, beauty. How's my girl?"

Caphy dropped to her haunches and whined softly, cocking her head.

"Who wants to play fetch?"

She leaped off the ground and went into a barking jag, her big paws stomping the floor inches from my feet.

I moved away from her deadly tail and sharp nails, bumping against the island at my back. "You shouldn't tease her," I shouted over the din. "She's going to be sitting in front of the door all night now."

"No, she's not. She's going to be in the car."

I frowned. "Is she taking a trip?"

Thankfully, Caphy stopped barking and dropped to her haunches again, her ears twitching.

"She is. You both are, actually."

I smiled, sliding onto a tall stool at the counter. "Oh yeah? Where exactly are we going, my dog and I?"

"Not far. But you'd better hurry. Your banana cream pie is getting wilty."

I surged to my feet, realizing what he was telling me. "You're here?"

"No. I'm *here*. You're *there*. We're currently bi-located. But I was hoping we could change that."

I hurried over and grabbed my keys off the hook on the wall, motioning to Caphy. It wasn't necessary. She was already bounding toward the garage door. "You're at *Sonny's*?"

Sonny's Diner served the best food in *Deer Hollow*, particularly the best banana cream pie. It was one of the places I hadn't been able to go into for days, since the construction crews discovered its existence and took it over.

"I'm not at the Diner. As soon as you're in your car I'll tell you where to go."

I ran up the stairs to my room, yanking my tee shirt off over my head as I ran. "I can't just start driving, Hal. You need to tell me where I'm heading."

"I will, once you get in the car."

I sighed with pretend pique. It didn't matter where he was taking me, I knew I'd love the trip and the arrival even more.

Ten minutes later, I opened the driver's side door of my 2012 Jeep Wrangler Sport, the car my parents had bought for me when I'd graduated High School. I still loved the car, though it was getting a bit long in the tooth. It had been my first car *and* a gift from my parents, giving it double nostalgia points

Caphy leaped in, bounding from the passenger side to the driver's side and hitting the horn with her butt. She leaped into the back seat in surprise as it went off.

I scolded her softly as I inserted my key. Then I dialed Hal's number and started speaking as I put the car into gear. "Okay, we're in the car, heading down the drive." Despite myself, I was getting excited. "I love scavenger hunts."

He laughed. "Well, on this hunt there are only two things to find. Me and this pie."

"Best scavenger hunt ever." I stopped at the end of the drive. "Which way on *Goat's Hollow*?"

"Left."

The plot thickened. There wasn't anything but countryside and a few remote homes in that direction. "I'm intrigued." As I headed down *Goat's Hollow*, I stared at a black Lincoln MKX parked on the side of the road, frowning. Nice car. Someone must have broken down. It would be a long walk to town.

"Take the first left."

I frowned. "*Pigs Wallow Lane*?"

"No. The left before that."

I slowed the car as I came upon a gravel driveway that was more dirt than gravel. Surely he didn't mean... "You're sure?"

"Yeah. Turn into the driveway and follow it until it ends. I'll be waiting there."

Okay, I was really confused. But realizing I was seconds

away from seeing my sexy PI, I didn't look a gift horse in the mouth. "See you soon."

I disconnected and jumped as a wide, pink tongue scoured my cheek. "Hey, girl. Hal's here."

As usual, my pibl read my excitement like a familiar novel. She yipped happily, spun once on the back seat and smashed her wide face into the window, looking for her favorite human male.

We bounced slowly and carefully along the rutted road. Tree branches that had grown since the last time we'd ventured down the neglected drive scraped the sides of my car and smacked against the windows.

Memories assailed me of being there before, looking for a childhood acquaintance who I thought might be dead. All we'd found that time was a dilapidated cabin that had recently been inhabited by the wrong guy.

Caphy spotted Hal before I did. He'd been leaning against a tree and I didn't see him until he straightened away from it. He had his hands shoved in the pockets of his black slacks. "Oh, Caphy, Hal's here."

She rammed herself into the door, yowling with excitement, her tail smacking the window behind her. It was all I could do to get the Jeep stopped next to Hal's big SUV before she pounded herself senseless against the frame.

I barely got the door open before she was leaping from the back seat, barreling toward Hal.

CHAPTER TWO

As always, my favorite private investigator looked edible. Usually swept straight back from a wide, unlined brow, his ink-black hair was slightly tousled, the late-day sun throwing off blue lights as it caressed the silky strands. He wore a pale green dress shirt that brought out the sexy olive tones in his skin and turned his dark green eyes the color of the pine trees at his back. The shirt sleeves were rolled to just below his elbows, accentuating the firm, muscular geography of his forearms.

As Caphy bounded in his direction, Hal's wide, kissable mouth spread in a happy smile, and he bent his six-feet-four-inch frame to pet her.

She sniffed his hand and then bounced straight into the air as he laughed. He was holding something behind his back. Whatever it was, my dog wanted it bad.

My gaze meeting his sexy dark green gaze, I knew exactly how she felt. "Hello, stranger."

His smile softened, and his gaze gained heat. "Hey, beautiful. You look positively delicious."

As it happened, I'd slipped and fallen into a flirty, flowery cotton dress on my way out the door to meet him. I might have been a bit underdressed as the sun dipped slowly behind the trees, but I had a feeling I wouldn't be cold for long.

Judging by the steamy look Hal was giving me, falling into the dress had been a happy accident.

"This old thing."

He laughed, dodging backward as Caphy, with the single-minded purpose only a pibl can have, vaulted into the air between us, yipping with excitement. "Okay, you win, beauty." He lifted the hand he held behind his back and showed her an orange tennis ball.

Caphy loves balls, and she seems to have a particular affection for those of the orange variety. I wasn't sure why. Maybe it was the smell of the dye in them or something. I didn't think dogs could even see color.

My beautiful blonde pitty didn't need to see the color. She barely even looked at the ball. As soon as she saw what it was, she was off and running toward the woods, turning her head with every other step to see when Hal launched it.

He didn't disappoint. His arm snapped out and the tennis ball flew high and long, into the copse of evergreens that towered over us in the near distance.

We watched her dive into the trees, grinning at her antics. I yelped as Hal reached out and snagged me around the waist, dragging me in for a kiss that made my toes curl in my flats.

A couple of minutes later, my mind muzzy and my body warm despite being underdressed, Hal broke the kiss and sighed as I rested my head on his chest. "I've missed you guys."

I bit my lip against the urge to tell him not to leave again. It was the perfect antidote to missing us when he went back home to Indianapolis. But I'd promised myself I wouldn't pressure him.

If he wanted to be with us more, he'd make the decision himself.

If he didn't...well...my pressuring him wasn't going to have a happy result. For either of us.

"Deep thoughts," he said, rubbing a fingertip along my jaw.

I forced a smile. "Nope. Not when I have pie waiting for me." I glanced around hopefully. "Where is it?"

He dropped his arm around my shoulders and we started walking away from the cars, toward the dilapidated cabin beyond the trees. "You'll see."

A soft breeze, scented with the smell of rich, black earth and pine needles, slipped past. I shivered slightly as something dark slid through me.

Hal rubbed my arm. "Are you cold?"

"No. I'm fine." But I didn't mind when he continued to rub his hand along my arm.

"Fall took a while to get here, but I don't think it will be here for long."

"No, it usually isn't, " I agreed. "Indiana seems to have given up on having four seasons. We pretty much just go from summer to winter and then back to summer again."

A soft crashing sound announced Caphy's return back through the piles of fallen leaves. She didn't even look at me. She shot like a rocket straight to Hal.

"Drop it," he told her. She worked the ball in her powerful jaws for a moment, clearly reluctant to let it go, and then finally dropped it slowly to the ground. Still, when he reached to pick it up, she dodged forward, tail wagging manically, and seemed to be struggling to keep herself from snatching it back.

Hal's hand closed over the soggy ball, and she flew away from him, tongue lolling.

"Ready?" he asked.

She barked, spinning around to grin at him before taking off like a shot. The ball sailed high and long again, disappearing behind a line of trees that were pretty enough for a painting. Dressed in fall colors of yellow, red and orange, the trees swayed gently with the breeze, depositing a soft rain of dry leaves over us as we moved past. "I'm dying to know why we're here."

Hal nodded. "I know."

I smacked his arm when he didn't elaborate.

He chuckled. "One more minute. You can wait that long, can't you?"

"Only because there's pie."

We walked in companionable silence for another minute, until the cabin came into view. The dark feeling swept through me again, quick as a thought, and my memories went reluctantly back to my last interaction with the cabin's owner. "I really hope Uncle Dev's not going to be on the other side of that cabin door."

Hal shook his head. The look he gave me was kind. "He's not here."

Devon Little wasn't really my uncle. He'd been my father's friend. They'd grown up together...worked together...and had been inseparable for most of their lives.

I'd known Devon for as long as I could remember.

Except I'd never really known him. I'd figured that out when a dead body turned up on my property, and he'd proven that his secrets were more important to him than I was. "Good." Then I frowned. "So, why are we here? I thought the cabin was for sale."

He gave me an enigmatic smile and tugged me into motion again. As we passed the rusty, broken down still where Uncle—I had to stop calling him that—Devon used to make his killer moonshine, I realized something was different.

The yard around the cabin was clean. No more chunks of rusty metal or pieces of broken glass and wood. The bushes had been trimmed and the leaves cleared from the front, a curving sidewalk of paving stones leading us to the front door.

"Nice," I said, pointing to the stones. "The Realtor's done a great job improving the curb appeal. Hal grinned, pulling open a brand-new storm door and whistling for Caphy.

She came loping toward us with the ball in her mouth, and bolted past Hal into the cabin. As he pushed the newly painted wood door into the interior of the home, I saw the warm glow of light flickering against the walls and floor.

I grabbed my cell phone.

"What are you doing?" Hal asked.

"Calling the fire department. I think the cabin's on fire."

Hal chuckled, tugging the phone from my hand. "Come on."

I stopped just inside the door, my awed gaze fixing on the round, wooden table across the room, which held two settings of fine china with silverware. A bottle of wine rested inside a bucket of ice. Two wine glasses sat next to it.

Silver candle holders held flickering tapers, the glow dancing over the warm wood of the floor and walls.

Across from the door, on the far wall, was a big stone fireplace which also held a fire. The sweet smell of burning wood wafted through the space, making it feel homey and safe.

A short leather couch faced the fireplace, and in front of it, repurposed iron and wood boxes held a large tray that was finished in a reddish gold stain that caught the flickering light of the fat candles arranged on its surface and turned it gold.

The aged beam mantle held another cluster of fat candles. Two more burned brightly on the stone hearth.

On either end of the couch were matching upholstered

chairs in a deep, rich red, the fabric covering knobby and inviting.

"Wow," I told him. I shook my head. "Dev's place looks great. But I don't understand. Why are we here?"

He walked over and poured champagne into the two glasses, handing me one. "To have dinner."

I slanted him a look and he tapped his glass against mine. "To christen the place."

I continued to stare at him for a moment longer, and then it finally sunk in. "You…" The words didn't want to leave my mouth. I frowned, sipped the golden, bubbly liquid in my glass to stall for time, and then tried again. "You…" Nope.

"I bought this place."

I continued to look at him, mute. I didn't really know how to react. Joy warred with irritation in my heart. On the one hand, his buying a home in *Deer Hollow* was terrific. It meant I'd see him more. It meant he was going to be right next door. It might even mean he was thinking that what we had was worth investing in. On the other hand, he hadn't even talked to me about it. Wasn't that something he should have done? Okay, we'd never talked about being a couple. Not really. We'd just enjoyed our time together. We'd kept it loose. Easy. But this…

"You're very quiet," he said, his handsome face starting to reflect concern.

I shrugged. "I can't believe you did all this without saying anything."

He nodded, settled the wine glass onto the table, and shoved his hands into his pockets. "I know. It probably seems like I was sneaking around behind your back…"

"Well, you were, weren't you?"

He winced. "I prefer to think of it as keeping a temporary secret. I wanted to surprise you."

"Well," I said, settling my glass next to his. "You certainly did that."

"You're not happy about this." It wasn't a question. I wasn't really good at hiding my feelings.

"I'm not sure what I am. Right now I'm feeling annoyed. I'll have to think about that for a bit and decide if that feeling is fair. In this moment, I think it is."

He reached out and touched my shoulder. "I understand."

Nodding, I called to Caphy. She jumped off the couch and trotted toward me, the tennis ball still clutched in her mouth. I pulled it out and gave it to him. It squished with slobber when I put it into his hand.

I fought a smile as he pulled a face.

"I think we should go." He didn't try to stop me as I headed toward the door. I was a little surprised by that. He didn't follow or call out to me as Caphy and I headed down the sidewalk and into the trees.

I was disappointed by that. But I couldn't really fault him for it. I was the one who was making a big thing out of his surprise, turning it into something negative.

I still wasn't sure if that was fair. I'd need to give myself some time to figure it out. And I couldn't think about his feelings while I did.

That would drag me too far off course.

My cell rang as I pulled up to my house. I answered as Caphy leaped out and ran happily toward the pond. "No swimming!" I called out to her.

She didn't appear to hear me. I knew that was on purpose. My pitty has a serious hearing problem. She seriously doesn't hear me when she doesn't want to.

I checked the ID and was disappointed it wasn't Hal. "Hey, Arno."

"Joey." As usual, the deputy sheriff was a man of as few words as he could get away with.

"What's up?"

"I have a report of a missing person."

I dropped down on the steps leading to my front porch and watched Caphy dance around the mucky edge of the pond. She liked to chase the three-foot-long fish that taunted her from the shallow water. I was going to have to hose off her feet and legs before she could go inside.

With my thoughts on Caphy's antics, it took me a moment to realize Arno had been speaking to me. "I'm sorry, what was that? Caphy's barking at that giant fish again and I didn't hear."

"I said there's a local real estate agent missing. Her name's Sellers."

"Penney Sellers?" I asked, frowning.

"That's her. Apparently, she left word at her office that she was coming out to your place. Nobody's seen or heard from her since."

"She was here. I sent her packing. That was only a couple of hours ago, Arno. She could just be running late."

"I told them the same thing. But, apparently, she missed a closing and that's unheard of for Ms. Sellers. She's kind of..." He hesitated as if looking for the right word.

"A shark?"

"I was going to say hungry...but your word works too."

"I take it you've met her?"

"I thought everyone had met Ms. Sellers. She's trying to get everybody in *Deer Hollow* to sell their homes."

I stood up and covered the phone with my hand, whistling to Caphy. "I'm devastated. I thought I was special."

"You *are* special, Joey. But just not with Ms. Sellers."

I snickered. "I hope you find her. She was annoying, but I wouldn't wish her any harm."

He sighed. "I guess I need to take a drive out your way. Hopefully, she didn't fall off the road at the park."

Deer County State Park was a thousand-acre extravaganza of trees and rocky ridges, with the agitated ribbon of *Fawn River* cutting through its rugged geography. The steepest ridges, dotted with coyote dens and hugging the most violent rapids of the river, bounded *Country Road 57* and had claimed more than a few careless drivers over the years.

"Good luck, Arno."

"Yeah. Talk to you later."

CHAPTER THREE

"Come on Caphy, girl!" My dog continued to ignore me, her front feet sunk ankle deep in muck near the waterlily patch in the pond.

"Cacophony!"

The full name thing brought her head around. She gave her tail a tentative wag and then started barking again, her gaze riveted to something in the midst of the lily pads.

"Leave that poor fish alone," I yelled, my footsteps taking on a stomping quality as she continued to ignore me.

"Bad girl, Caphy." I rounded the pond and my gaze slid to the floating flowers, looking for signs of the big fish that roamed the pond like a shark. I didn't see any sign of her watery nemesis.

But what I did see made my pulse stutter and shoot skyward.

A brown squirrel's nest floated among the lilies, a few loose strands drifting away from the nest to cling to the velvet beauty of the flowers nearby. A few feet from the nest, a pale hand rested against a half-submerged log. The pale, slightly waterlogged knuckles appeared scraped and one stubby fingernail was broken below the quick.

With a yelp of recognition, I skidded to a halt.

Caphy stopped barking and dropped to her haunches, her pretty green gaze locked on me to gauge my reaction. I started to call her to me, but my throat closed on the words. I cleared it and tried again, my voice coming out in a husky wheeze.

She gave an uncertain wag of her tail and whined.

"Come on, girl. You need to listen to me." I wasn't sure what I was most worried about...the idea my dog would grab hold of the corpse in my pond, or the thought that it would sink into the muck and be lost.

I needed to call Arno. "Caphy, come!" The command came out harsher than I'd planned, and my dog's head drooped, her ears flattening against her wide head. She whined pitifully.

"I'm sorry," I told her gently. "Come see me, pretty girl."

She pulled her muck-laden legs from the pond and slunk over, dropping to her belly at my feet. Her drama had the intended effect on me. Guilt turned my stomach to acid as I reached down and pulled her squishy face to mine, giving her a kiss in the wide space between her eyes. "That's a good girl."

Immediately appeased, Caphy jumped up and started hopping around me, grinning maniacally as I walked away from the pond, drawing her with me.

I dialed Arno's number and waited for it to ring.

The call never went through.

Before he answered it, I heard the crunch of car tires on gravel and looked up to find his radio car rolling slowly along my drive.

I flagged him down and he stopped midway along the drive, climbing out of the car and striding toward me on long legs covered in tan uniform slacks.

He wore the big hat well, the brim shadowing his handsome face, which I knew would be taut with intensity. It was his cop face.

He spoke into his phone as he approached and disconnected before he got close enough for me to hear. He stopped beside me, bending slightly to give my dog a scratch between her ears. "Caphy girl."

She swiped a wide tongue over his wrist in response.

He straightened, removing aviator sunglasses that hid his eyes and fixing me with the look I'd known I'd see. "Joey."

"Arno," I responded, falling into teasing mode by habit. But I immediately caught myself and pointed toward the pond. "I think I've found your Penney Sellers."

Arno's intense gaze skimmed over the pond, landing on the floating corpse. He didn't look surprised. "Looks like." He frowned. "You didn't muck up the scene, did you?"

I would have been shocked at the seemingly unsympathetic joke, but I knew he sometimes used humor to deal with the more gruesome aspects of his job. "Har. No, the muck was already there. But Caphy's paw prints are embedded deeply in the scene. Do you want her to give you her prints so you can eliminate her as a suspect?"

His lips twitched slightly. "You're assuming she's not my main suspect in this."

Caphy's gaze went from Arno to me as we spoke, looking for all the world as if she was watching a tennis match.

"She had no motive," I told him. "Unlike me, she didn't really dislike the woman. Though I have no idea why."

Arno lifted a golden eyebrow. "Do I need to look at you for this?"

"If you're picking your suspect according to who doesn't like her, you're going to have a lot of suspects."

He sighed. "That's what I'm afraid of." He glanced at Caphy. "Keep her here."

I nodded as he moved over to the pond and crouched down near the edge, his gaze gliding over Penney Seller's buoyant body and then toward the woods. He straightened a moment later and walked around the pond, his gaze scouring the ground as he walked.

He stopped about ten yards away and stared off into the woods, toward the road.

"You didn't tell me why you stopped by," I called out to him.

He ignored me for a moment and then pulled out his cell, making a phone call as he worked his way back to where Caphy and I waited. After he hung up, he finally looked at me, pulling the big, brown hat off his head and mopping his forehead with the sleeve of his uniform shirt. Though it was early Fall and the sun was low in the sky, it was still hot enough to bring a gloss to the skin of anybody who dared to move around very much. He jerked his head toward the woods. "I found Ms. Sellers' car parked along *Goats Hollow Road*, through the woods there."

"Do you suppose she slipped and fell in, hit her head on something?"

"I'd rather not speculate. The ME will do her work and then we'll know."

I'd known he was going to go that route. Arno believed words were unnecessary things which all too often caused him to be inconvenienced. I'd known him since grade school, and that had pretty much been his operating system even then.

"Did you notice that broken nail there? The bruised knuckles?"

Arno frowned and crossed his arms over his chest. He wasn't going to talk about the body with me.

Dangit! I had an unnatural curiosity that inconvenienced *me*. No wonder Arno and I got along like oil and water.

Distant sirens split the silence. Arno's peeps were on their way. He jerked his head at me. "You and Caphy go on inside."

"I'd like to stay."

"Not gonna happen, Joey. You take your dog inside and stay out of the way."

"I have to hose off her legs."

He cringed at the black muck clinging to my dog's blonde fur. "Yes, you definitely do."

I tugged Caphy's collar, silently happy that, for once, her messy ways were going to work in my favor. I was thinkin' that hosing off her stocky legs might take longer than anybody expected.

A whole lot longer.

Two hours later, the body was being rolled toward the waiting ambulance, ensconced in a body bag, and Arno was over-seeing the placing of crime scene tape around the area.

I frowned when I saw how much of it they were stringing up, using the trees to hold it in a more-or-less uniform shape that encompassed most of my pond.

I was about half afraid they were going to pluck the fish and turtles out of the water and tape evidence markers onto them.

My phone rang, and I glanced down. It was Hal. Though it went against my deepest desire, I hit *Ignore*. It wasn't only because I was annoyed with him at the moment. It was also because, if I talked to him, I'd have to tell him about the body in my pond. And Hal being Hal, he'd drop whatever he was doing and come rushing over to make sure Caphy and I were okay.

While that wasn't all bad in itself, I wasn't sure I was

ready to deal with him being nice to me. I was still too busy being ticked.

Though, I really wished I had somebody to chat with about the new development in my chamber of horrors. I thought about that for a moment and then grinned. I knew just the person to call.

My cousin Felicity Chance answered the phone on the third ring. "What have you done to Hal?"

I winced. I should have known Felly would get the news faster than the speed of gossip. "I didn't do anything to him. Why?"

"Cal just talked to him, and he said his brother sounded like somebody had stomped on his heart and ground it to dust."

I rolled my eyes. "Drama much?"

She sighed. "What can I say, men are hopeless drama queens. But really. Did you two have a fight?"

"Sort of." I fought a wave of frustration. I hadn't called my cousin to discuss my wobbly love life. "Look, I don't want to talk about it."

A beat of silence broadcasted Felly's displeasure with my statement. I let the silence sit between us for two more beats and then gave in. "He bought a house...a cabin really...in *Deer Hollow*.

"And that's bad, why? I thought you wanted him closer so you could see him more."

"It's not bad. Exactly."

"You're not making any sense, Joe."

I sighed. "I know. That's why I didn't want to talk about it. I'm not even sure myself why I'm mad at him."

"Is it because he didn't discuss it with you first?"

Relief filled me. My cousin knew me so well. "We not only didn't discuss it...he's been spending time here without telling me. Getting the cabin ready to move into."

She gave a long, drawn-out sigh. "Let me guess. He said he wanted to surprise you?"

"I was surprised, all right." I chewed the inside of my lip and thought for a moment, my gaze pointed toward the activity at the pond but not really seeing it. "I can't shake the feeling he didn't tell me because he wanted to leave himself an out. In case he changed his mind."

"That's a guy thing." I could almost hear her shaking her head with disgust. "Okay. I understand. Now, what else is going on?" She laughed brightly. "At least you're not calling to tell me you found another body, right?"

I winced again. Now that I had her on the phone, I realized what a mistake it had been to call her. She'd really freaked the last time I'd called to tell her I'd found a dead guy in my woods. She was going to go all, fiercely-protective-Felly on me when I told her there was another one. "Um..."

"Oh no, Joe! Really?"

"You can't tell Cal!" I chirped out quickly.

"Why not?" Her question came out in a warbly whine.

"Because he'll tell Hal, and I don't want him to know."

"Honey, he's going to find out. It's not like finding a body in *Deer Hollow* happens every day. That local rag you call a paper's going to barf it out in five-inch high letters on the front page."

Ugh! She was right. And with the current attention being paid to the *Hollow* because of the whole "Best Place to Live" thing, it was just as likely to hit the Indianapolis papers too. "I don't want him to feel obligated to help me."

"Now you're just being stupid. Whatever's going on in Hal's beady little man brain, you have to know he's crazy about you and your dog."

"Yeah, sometimes I think he loves Caphy more than he likes me."

Hearing her name spoken, Caphy's eyes popped open. She

lifted her head off my lap, her tongue bathing the boards of the front porch a couple of times before she flopped back into my lap with a sigh.

"Now you're just being ridiculous."

I expelled air in a rush. I knew she was right. But I was indulging in a pity party for one. I chuckled when I realized what I'd said. With a pibl in my lap, I actually was indulging in a 'pitty' party. "I know."

"So what's up with the body you found. Please tell me it isn't on your property this time."

"I wish I could."

"Bleurgh! Where was it this time?"

"The pond. Floating among the lily pads."

"Who was it?"

"A real estate agent named Penney Sellers." I grinned when Felly barked out a laugh.

"Seriously?"

"Dead serious," I said, my grin widening. "She knocked on my door earlier today, asking if I wanted to sell my house."

"Oh, oh. What did you say?"

"I said thanks but no thanks. The last time I saw her alive was just before I slammed the door in her face."

"Yikes! You fought with the deceased?"

Frowning, I started to argue and realized she was right. "I wouldn't call it a fight, really. But she's...she was a very forceful person. When I told her no, she tried to push me into selling the land so she could cut it up into five-acre lots."

"Yeah, that's pretty pushy." She hesitated a beat before asking, "Is Arno Willager, my favorite Villager, looking askance at you? Like he thinks you offed the poor thing?"

"Not yet. But give him time."

She sighed again. "Okay, I'm coming down there."

"What? No! At least not with the misguided notion that I

need help. If you want to come help me shame Hal into next week, that's another issue."

She laughed. "I could do that. But I'm more worried about your safety. Who killed this woman, and why did it happen on your property?" Then she sucked air. "Joe, you don't suppose...?"

She didn't need to finish the thought. It had already occurred to me. "Devon didn't kill her."

"How do you know?"

"Because..." My response trickled away as I realized I didn't really have a good reason why I thought that. The man had proven himself capable of almost anything. "I don't even know if he's around. He hasn't shown back up since that whole thing at the auction. Why would he suddenly involve himself in this?"

"I'm just spitballing here, but Dev was always pretty adamant about protecting your dad. What if he saw this Realtor sniffing around as an assault on Uncle Brent's memory somehow? He'd want you to stay in that house. It keeps your parents' memories alive."

That made a twisted kind of sense. "Maybe. But I'm sure Arno's already thought of that."

"Probably," Felly said dejectedly. "Are you sure you don't want my help? I wouldn't mind sinking my teeth into another mystery. I'm suffering from winter doldrums."

I laughed. "It's not even winter yet, Felly. In fact, it's barely fall."

"Still... I might need to go purse shopping to drag myself out of it." I could hear the smile in her voice. My cousin loved nothing more than a good purse. She had a closet full of them in all shapes, colors, styles, and sizes.

"I love you. But I'm going to let Arno handle this. He's a good cop. He'll get to the bottom of it."

"Okay, honey. I love you too. Talk to you soon?"

"Absolutely."

I hung up and lifted my gaze toward the remaining activity down by my pond. The ambulance had left, its lights and sirens inactive and silent. There was obviously no need for speed with poor Penney Sellers.

Arno opened the door of his radio car and lifted a hand to let me know he was leaving. I waved back and sat in thoughtful silence as he backed into the grass and turned, following the other deputies out onto *Goats Hollow Road*.

My mind replayed my first and last interaction with the dead realtor, wondering if there'd been any indication she was worried or upset. I didn't remember anything.

The woman had seemed confident and uncomfortably aggressive, as if she feared nothing but missing out on a sale.

Maybe her killer had snuck up on her. Maybe she'd unwittingly irritated the wrong person and paid the ultimate price. Or maybe she'd seen or heard something she shouldn't have. I discounted that last option because of where she'd been killed. I was pretty sure there were no lethal goings on down by my pond.

Not unless you counted Caphy's friend the big fish eating tadpoles as deadly intrigue.

I shook my head, pushing Caphy gently off my lap to stand. "Come on, girl. Let's eat something. I'm starving."

She jumped up and galloped through the front door, which I'd left slightly ajar in case we needed to make a quick retreat.

I reminded myself that I'd promised to let Arno do his job. To stay out of it as I should have done the last time. But even as I reminded myself of that, I decided it wouldn't hurt to pay a visit to Penney Seller's office in the morning.

Then I'd pass anything I learned off to Arno. Right away.

Sure I would.

CHAPTER FOUR

Deer Hollow Realtors was located in an old brick building that looked a little bit like what I thought the saloon in a town from the Wild West might look like.

The brick covering its front was stained black with age and, as I approached along a flagstone walkway, I noticed the rectangular building's façade was cracked in several spots, the fissures carelessly filled in with what looked like instant concrete.

The front porch was probably the newest thing on the building, and it looked to be older than I was. The wood planks were warped and gray with age, the supports splintered and shaped like an old lady's arthritic limbs.

The frames around the windows had been painted white once upon a time. They were currently so chipped they were mostly fossilized dark green paint with the occasional speckle of white paint still clinging desperately to the mottled surface.

The sign hanging from a metal arm attached to one of the two columns on either side of the steps was dented, the black letters of the business name pitted and stretched as if someone had once twisted it to see if the letters would pop off.

I headed for the flimsy wood storm door and pulled it open. It whined pitifully, and one corner caught on the warped porch boards. I left it wedged there and opened the front door, which was painted a dark burgundy and looked festive under a fall-colored wreath.

Sticking my head inside, I called out before entering. "Hello?"

There was a brief silence and then some scuffling sounds that almost made me back out again. It sounded as if I'd interrupted something.

A woman emerged from a door across the room, weaving her way through the three desks filling the small space. She shoved at a thick mop of dark hair on top of her head. "Hey, hon. Can I help you?"

The woman looked to be in her forties. She was plump and pretty in a careworn way, and I'd bet Caphy's last dog cookie she'd been in a clinch with somebody when I knocked on the door. Along with the telltale tousled hair, her lipstick painted the skin around her lips, and her blouse hung crookedly beneath her cardigan sweater, one button off from being straight.

I stepped through the door, giving her a quick smile. "Hi. I'm Joey Fulle. I live outside of town, off *Goat's Hollow Road*."

The woman's eyes lit up. "Oh yes. I'm familiar with that area. It's beautiful up there."

I struggled to place her. Though she was probably fifteen years older than I was, I should have known her. I knew most of the people in my little town. And for the ones I didn't know, I generally knew someone they were related to or friends with.

Such is the reality of a small town.

Unfortunately, I was pretty sure I'd never met the woman standing before me.

She offered me her hand, the other hand tugging at the bottom of her blouse in an effort to pull it straight. "I'm Madge Watson. It's a pleasure to meet you, Joey."

A door closed loudly at the back of the building and my gaze shot in that direction.

Madge took a step toward me, drawing my attention away from the door. "What brings you into *Deer Hollow Realtors*, hon?"

I let my gaze drift slowly back to her face, and her smile tightened slightly. She obviously didn't want me to speculate on the person who'd just left through the back door. "I wanted to tell you how sorry I was about Penney Sellers. She was found on my property, I'm afraid."

Madge's pale blue gaze widened in surprise. "Oh, my! I didn't realize." She clasped my hand in both of hers. Her skin was like ice. "You found her, didn't you?"

I nodded.

She squeezed my fingers. "That must have been horrible for you." Her eyes lit with excitement that I found just a tad disconcerting.

"It wasn't pleasant, for sure. But I just wanted to give you my sympathies. I'm sure it must be quite a shock."

"Oh, it is. It's just horrible. Of course, I didn't know Penney all that well. Like me, she came to *Deer Hollow* from another real estate agency in Indy. We've only known each other for a few weeks."

I nodded. "Then I guess you wouldn't have any idea who might have wanted to hurt her?" I realized, too late, that the realtor might take offense to my inappropriate curiosity. I needn't have worried. She seemed just as curious about her fellow realtor's death as I did.

"No. I've thought a lot about it since that cute Deputy

Willager came to tell me she was gone. There's just nobody.
Everybody loved Penney."

I fought to keep surprise from showing on my face. Even
if Arno hadn't told me the dead woman had been ruffling
feathers all over town, I'd have known it just by being around
her for a few minutes.

Penney Sellers could easily have swum as head shark in a
tank filled with deadly sharks. Her behavior at my house had
proved her to be relentless. I'd shooed her away in no uncertain terms, yet she'd snuck back onto my property shortly
after I'd left and had gotten herself killed there.

With a start, I realized she had to have been watching my
house. She'd probably seen me leave and had taken advantage
of my absence to snoop around.

I struggled to find a way around Madge's obvious lie about
Penney's popularity. Finally, I settled for presenting my own
experience with her. "She'd seemed very determined to me.
Speaking as someone who knows this community really well,
that kind of doggedness can sometimes ruffle feathers."

"Oh yes, that's certainly true. But Penney was very good
with people. She had a way of getting what she wanted and
leaving people feeling as if they were the winners."

I wondered if she and I were talking about the same
woman. "Penney Sellers?"

She nodded, oblivious to my skepticism.

"Maybe somebody from Indianapolis had it out for her?"

"If so, Penney never mentioned it."

"Was she married?"

Shaking her head, Madge finally seemed to clue in on my
nosiness. "Are you a cop?"

I laughed in what I hoped was a dismissive way, forcing a
smile. "Not a chance. I was just wondering...you know...since
she was killed on my land. It's made me feel a little unsafe.
You know what I mean?"

It was a dirty trick, playing the weak woman card, but I couldn't have Madge clamming up on me because she thought I was too nosy.

She patted my arm, making sympathetic noises. "I don't think you have to worry about one of Penney's old flames coming after you. From what I could tell, she didn't have any romantic interests at all. She pretty much lived for her job." Madge frowned, lifting a finger. "There was this one guy. I think he was a new client. They had a pretty wild fight here in the office yesterday morning."

That sounded promising. "Violent?"

She shrugged. "No idea. I came out of the restroom and saw them standing over there by the coffee machine. I cleared out when I heard them arguing. I'm not fond of confrontation." She flushed with embarrassment. "I had an appointment across town."

"What did this guy look like?"

"Tall guy. Looked good from the back. But I couldn't see his face."

"Local?"

"I couldn't tell you. Most of our clients are people wanting to move into town, so we mostly deal with outsiders."

I nodded. "If you see him again will you call me?"

She shrugged. "Sure."

I grabbed a pen from the nearby desk and jotted my number on an old-fashioned, stained and torn paper blotter. "Is there anything else you can tell me about Penney?"

Madge pursed her lips thoughtfully. "She had a cat. But I don't think LaLee is a danger to you." She grinned.

"Oh no. Poor thing. Who will take care of her?"

Madge flipped a hand into the air. "No idea. I don't really care, either. I hate cats."

My lip curled. I looked away to hide my disgust. People with such a cavalier attitude toward animals rubbed me the wrong way. "I'd like to stop by and get the cat. I'll take her someplace where she'll be safe. Can you give me Penney's address?"

The woman frowned. "I'm sure someone will put the nasty thing in a kennel and take it to the pound."

And that was exactly what I was afraid of. "You know, Madge, I've lived in *Deer Hollow* all my life. I know just about everybody here..." I let the statement slide off into silence, hoping she'd take my meaning. The wrong word in the right ears would go far toward cutting into Madge's business. By contrast, if I vouched for her...

The woman gave me an insincere smile. "You're right, of course. Penney loved that stu...cat like it was a child. She'd want someone to make sure it was safe." Madge reached for a pad of yellow stickies and jotted down an address. Then she opened the desk drawer and pulled out a key on an expandable wristband. "Penney always kept a spare key in her desk. She tended to lock herself out a lot."

I took the key and the sticky, turning toward the door.

"Be careful. That cat's pure evil. You might want to go in armed or something."

Not bothering to hide my frown, I made a quick getaway. Madge's warning didn't bother me a whit. She clearly didn't like cats. And I was looking forward to the chance to search Penney's house, thinking that maybe I'd find something which would shine some light on who might have killed the realtor. Saving poor LaLee from neglect and starvation would be a bonus.

I bounced happily down the steps and headed for my car in the small, gravel side lot.

Five steps later I screeched to a halt, my gaze locking onto the lean, handsome figure leaning against my car.

Dangit!

CHAPTER FIVE

"What are you doing, Joey?"

My hackles rose, and I fought the defensive words flying to my lips. "I can ask you the same thing. What are you doing here?"

Hal held my gaze for a long moment and then shifted away from my car, striding toward me like a tiger stalking its prey. "I asked you first."

Oh, so that was how he was going to play it. "I was just talking to a realtor. You know all about that, huh? I just found out recently that *you've* been talking to one too." I let my eyebrows lift in feigned surprise. "Was Penney Sellers the one who sold you your new house? Maybe you even told her about me. Is that why she came to harass me at my home?"

His expression darkened. "Joey..."

"No, it's okay. You can just tell me if you sicced her on me. I'll add it to the growing list of things I'm annoyed at you about. We might as well get it all out. You know, clear the air."

"Joey..."

I lifted a hand and stepped around him. "No, don't bother.

I get it. You wanted to keep your options open. You know...in case you decided you really didn't want to spend more time with me after all..."

His hand snaked out and wrapped around my arm, drawing me gently to a halt. "How did this become a discussion about me buying that house?"

Because I'd needed to distract you.

The thought almost made me smile. Instead, I shrugged, tugging my arm free. "It isn't. But you know, that's probably the problem. I'm talking about our relationship and you think I'm talking about you buying a stupid house."

He turned and fell into step with me, his long strides easily keeping up as I hurried toward my car. "Why didn't you tell me about the dead woman on your property?"

I jerked to a stop, not bothering to hide my annoyance. "How did you find out about that?"

He lifted a midnight eyebrow. "Really?"

Okay, he had me there. The *Deer Hollow* gossip tree was flappin' in the wind, dropping tidbits of juicy information all over the dang place. "You talked to your brother?"

"No." He frowned. Are you saying that Cal knew about this, but nobody told me?"

Oops!

"I told Felly. I figured she'd tell him. But I told her not to."

He shook his head. "I ran into Arno at the diner. He told me."

So much for keeping the investigation quiet. "For a cop, he sucks at keeping things close to the vest."

Hal's lips twitched with humor. "He wanted me to know so I could keep you safe."

My hackles rose again. "There are so many things wrong with that statement."

He sighed, dipping his head and crossing his arms over his chest. "Go on, smack me around. Let's get this over with so we can move forward with finding out who killed this poor woman."

My mouth snapped shut and I blinked. "You're investigating Penney Seller's murder?"

"Her death, yes. I told Arno I couldn't just sit around and wait to find out if you were in danger."

I sighed. I'd known he'd feel compelled to ride to the rescue. "I'm fine. You don't need to..."

He tapped my lips with a warm fingertip. "Save your breath. I made Caphy a promise, and I'm going to keep it."

I sighed. Sure, he'd make my dog promises. With me, he left his options open. "What promise? That you'd play ball with her later?"

"That I'd keep you safe and make you happy."

I fought a grin. "She wrung that out of you, did she?"

"In her own way, yes." He grinned and I felt its effects like a punch to the belly.

I needed to change the subject fast. "I'm surprised Arno's letting you stick your Greek nose into this."

"He's got his hands full with that meth lab massacre and the school bus hit and run."

Ice filled my chest. The meth lab thing had broken a few days earlier. Three people had been shot, execution style, in a ramshackle house out in the country. Arno'd had his hands full trying to find out how and why they were killed. The school bus thing had happened just the night before. Someone had hit the driver of a bus, who'd climbed out of the vehicle to help a special needs kid in a wheelchair onto the loading ramp at the back of the bus.

I shook my head. "What's going on in our little town?" I murmured, before realizing I'd momentarily forgotten Hal wasn't really a *Deer Hollow*-er.

That thought gave me pause. Since he'd bought Dev's cabin, would he really be one of us?

"*Penney* for your thoughts," Hal said on a grin.

I couldn't help smiling. "I see what you did there."

He chuckled.

I sighed. "Okay, let's put this cabin thing behind us for now. I was just heading over to Ms. Sellers' house to see what I can find. Plus, I understand she has a cat. I'm going to make sure the animal is taken care of."

Hal nodded. "Sounds like a plan. Your car or mine?"

Penney Sellers had lived in an old church that was transformed into a home. Slightly outside of town, the white, clapboard building looked like just about every other country church, with a spired roofline and windows with rounded tops and stained glass.

The gravel parking lot at the side had been turned into a rock garden, with pathways created by different colored stones and slate pavers winding between raised flower beds and the occasional twisty bush or decorative tree. A fountain and pond were the centerpiece of the space, the water splashing gently over a complex array of variously-sized and shaped rocks.

Koi fish swam and darted in the watery depths of the architecturally stunning fountain.

"This is pretty," I told Hal as I stepped out of his car.

He eyed the fountain, his dark green gaze narrowing. "I'm apparently in the wrong business. There must be a ton of money in real estate."

He was right, of course. The landscaping we were looking at probably cost Penney Sellers tens of thousands of dollars to create. And I had a suspicion the inside of the unique home was going to be equally impressive.

I wasn't wrong.

I used the key Madge had given me to unlock the front door. We stepped out of the crisp fall temps into the warm but slightly musty interior of the home.

Golden oak floors gleamed at us from under expensive looking oriental rugs. My shoes sunk into the thick rugs when I stepped on them, confirming they were likely as pricey as they looked.

High above our heads, a stainless steel and crystal chandelier caught the early morning sunlight and cast it over the stark, white walls in pretty, dancing patterns.

The main room was unbroken, with only furniture and rugs to delineate sections of space. Two antique church pews, covered in colorful pillows, sat at right angles to each other in front of a brick fireplace, which was painted gray. Dozens of candles of varying sizes and shapes lined up on the heavy, antique mantle, most of them sporting thick ribbons of melted wax along their misshapen sides. They were obviously not just for show. Ms. Sellers must have liked a little ambiance.

Angled on the other side of the fireplace, was a gray leather recliner that looked as if I would sink into it up to my eyebrows if I sat down. "I'd have to lure Caphy out of that recliner with food. She'd never leave it otherwise."

Hal chuckled. "That's not a lie."

We shared a smile about my goofy dog. For a moment, I felt the easy comradery of parents tied together by the antics of their child.

It didn't really matter if the child was a pibl.

Not to me anyway.

I turned toward the kitchen area, which was located one deep step up from the living area at the farthest point from the front door. I realized that would have been where the altar was when the building was still a church.

Simple Shaker-style cabinets, in the same golden oak as the floors, filled the entire back wall. The cabinets housed gleaming stainless-steel appliances and framed an aged copper farm sink in the center. The countertops appeared to be speckled black concrete, that looked a little bit like granite. A huge island filled the center of the space, and four tall iron stools were tucked under the counter on the living room side. The window over the sink was clear glass, but its shape matched the round-topped windows at the front of the building. Beyond the glass, I could make out a big tree whose leaves were painted with fall colors, and a lot of green grass.

The "bedroom" was located on the left-hand side of the space, along with a large master bath that appeared to have been built into what was probably the pastor's office. The king-sized bed and two dressers were partitioned off from the rest of the space by beautiful, oriental-style privacy panels along one side.

"Wow," I said, looking around. "Either Ms. Sellers was selling drugs, or she was a darn good realtor."

Hal didn't respond. His expression remained speculative.

After a moment, he moved toward the kitchen. "You search the bedroom. I'll take the kitchen."

Nodding, I headed toward the partitioned space and started rifling through the drawers of Penney Sellers' long, dark wood dresser and the two nightstands. I found a cheap cardboard journal buried under Penney's socks and pulled it out. Opening it, I figured I'd find some kind of personal diary. Instead, I found a long list of addresses with the value of each property in a column next to the address and another dollar amount next to that one. It appeared to be a list of homes Penney Sellers had sold. But I had no explanation for the second dollar amount. Or the check mark next to some of the homes but not others. Maybe those were homes she'd sold, and the unchecked ones were homes she either hadn't sold yet or had lost the contract for at some point.

I scanned quickly through the pages, discovering that the last two pages contained addresses I recognized in *Deer Hollow*.

To my shock, I noted the address of *Sonny's Diner* on the second to the last page. My stomach twisted with alarm and I made a soft sound of concern.

"What did you find?" Hal asked. He stood at the end of the partition, his hands shoved into his pockets.

Apparently, he hadn't found anything.

I held the journal up and he walked over, taking it from my hand. "*Sonny's Diner* is on the market?"

His gaze shot to mine. "I can't believe Max would sell the place. It's been in her family for generations."

"I know." I wrapped my arms around myself, feeling suddenly as if someone had walked over my grave. I shuddered. "*Deer Hollow* is changing, and it makes me sad."

"Let's not jump to conclusions." He flipped through to the last page and went very still, the color leaching from his handsome face.

"What is it?" I asked him, moving around to look at the page he was staring at. It didn't take long for me to find it. "Uh, uh. That's not right."

He slowly closed the journal, his shoulders rigid. "Is there something you forgot to tell me?"

Irritation flared. I wasn't the one keeping real estate secrets. "I have no idea why my house is on that list. It must be a list of homes she hopes to contract."

"Then how do you explain the second dollar amount?"

"I have no idea. But I can assure you that even if Penney Sellers had sold my home she wouldn't have gotten a $250,000 fee from it."

Understanding flared in his dark green gaze and Hal slowly relaxed. "You're right."

"I don't know what those numbers are, but they're too high to represent Real Estate Commisions."

Hal nodded.

"Yeow!"

A gray-brown blur shot past Hal's legs, and he yelped as the critter clamped onto his calf with razor sharp teeth and then shot away as he swung a hand in its direction.

Hal's attacker dove under the bed. A throaty growl was all the evidence we had that we'd even seen the cat.

"I'm guessing you just met LaLee," I told him, hiding a smile behind my hand.

"It bit me!" he exclaimed in shock.

My grin widened. "I guess she doesn't like strangers in her house."

His midnight brows lowered. "You're an intruder too, and it didn't bite you."

I shrugged. "I'll see if I can find a crate and try to entice her into it."

"Yeah," he grumbled, rubbing his calf. "Good luck with that."

I pulled open a door on the wall dividing the bathroom from the bedroom and found a large, walk-in closet. Flipping on the light, I cast a look over my shoulder. "Can you check the kitchen for some tuna or something to bribe her with?"

Hal limped around the partition, grumbling under his breath. I'm pretty sure it was something about needing a rabies shot.

CHAPTER SIX

"What do you mean you won't take her?" I yelled at Arno.

"I'm sorry, Joey. You need to call the pound. I'm not set up to rehome people's pets."

"I'm not asking you to rehome her. I just need someone to foster her until I can find her a place to live."

"Not gonna happen. I guess you're going to have to foster the cat yourself. Gotta go."

I slammed my phone against my thigh as Arno disconnected in my ear.

"No luck?" Hal asked. I glanced his way, grimacing at the bloody claw tracks decorating his square jaw.

"No." I rubbed a matching set of tracks on my forearm and winced as I moved my leg and was reminded of the bite wounds around my ankle. "I can't keep this cat in my house. Caphy will have a cow and five ducks."

"On the upside, maybe she'll eat it."

"That's not funny."

His midnight brows arched. "Why do you think I was kidding?"

Shaking my head, I turned to stare out the window for a minute, thinking. There was really only one solution.

I turned back to Hal and fixed him with a pleading look. He lifted both hands off the wheel, his head shaking violently. "Not a chance. That thing's a demon come straight from Hell. Plus, it hates me. There's no way I'm taking it in."

A deep, throaty growl emerged from the soft-sided kennel in the back seat. Hal had insisted on putting the kennel in the third row of seating in the big car, as if he were afraid the cat would reach out of the kennel and scratch us through the seats.

After going a few rounds with the cranky Siamese cat, I wasn't at all sure he was wrong. "I'll give you that she's not very trusting..."

He barked out a laugh that sounded slightly wheezy.

"But she's probably terrified. Put yourself in her...erm... paws. We invaded her home and put her into a kennel. Now we're taking her away from everything she knows."

Hal stared straight ahead for a long moment, his eyes on the road but his thoughts clearly somewhere else. Finally, he nodded. "I can understand all that. I can even kind of, sort of, forgive the cat for the scratches. But I still can't take her." He reached up and scratched at the claw marks on his chin, which I saw had gotten even redder and looked puffier than before. In fact, that whole side of his face was swollen. "Are you okay?"

"I'm fine. But I need to drop you off at your house and get to the hospital. There's a better than medium chance I'm going to go into anaphylactic shock."

I squealed in alarm. "Why didn't you tell me? Go right now! Don't go to my house, just head straight to the hospital."

My voice had gained a shrieking quality that was not only unattractive, but it was apparently alarming to LaLee. She started yowling and thrashing around in the kennel. I forced myself to calm down. "It's okay, LaLee. Relax, girl."

Hal scratched his forearm, where two puncture holes had blown up to three times the size they'd been at Penney Seller's house. "Maybe you should pull over and let me drive."

He shook his head. "I'm okay. Just itchy and...puffy." He threw me a grin.

Since the swelling in his face had grown to alarming proportions, that was the understatement of the century. "You might want to drive faster."

For once, he didn't argue. He flew past the turnoff to my house and headed straight for *Deer Hollow General Hospital*.

I sat in a nearly empty waiting room while they hurried Hal back to a private room in Emergency.

Down by my feet, LaLee had given up thrashing around and had her expressive face pressed against the "window" of the kennel, peering around the waiting room. I hadn't been able to leave the traumatized feline in the car by herself, despite the fact I had to dodge a few swipes of her razor-sharp claws on the way. "Now don't make me regret bringing you inside, LaLee. Be good."

The cat's answer was a deep-throated growl that didn't sound very appreciative of my efforts to keep her safe.

"Is that a new addition to your house, Joey?"

I glanced up to find an old schoolmate coming toward me, a wide smile on her plain face. Sally Winthrop was wearing the loose, cotton scrubs of a surgical nurse and she had a mask hanging around her neck. She looked as if she'd just come out of surgery.

"Hey, Sally." I returned her smile. "This cat's owner died, and I'm just caring for her until I can find her a new home.

You're not in the market for a Siamese cat by any chance, are you?"

"Not today, no." She sat down next to me and stuck her finger through one of the openings on the side. "Aren't you a pretty thing."

"You probably shouldn't..."

LaLee batted playfully at the finger but didn't draw blood. I said a prayer of thanks and tried to distract my friend from offering human shish kabob to the killer cat. "She belonged to Penney Sellers. The woman whose body they fished out of my pond."

Sally frowned. "Ah. Yes. I was here when they brought the body in." She gave me a worried look. "Are you okay? Finding bodies is getting to be a regular thing for you, isn't it?"

"I'm fine. I just don't understand why she was killed at my place."

"She was a realtor, right? Maybe she stopped by to check out your property..." Sally shrugged. "I understand she'd been trying to get a lot of people to sell their houses."

"You see, that's just the thing. She did stop by, and I sent her packing. I watched her leave."

"That is strange. But from what I heard, I wouldn't put it past her. Your property is one of the nicest in the area. I'm betting she wouldn't let it go without a fight."

I sighed. "You know, Sal, I supported this new subdivision at first. I thought it would bring in some new blood...maybe a few new businesses...but I'm starting not to like the effects of it."

Sally gave me a weary glance. "I hear ya, sister. With all the construction folks and the looky-loos tramping around *Deer County State Park* and breaking bones and stuff, we've never been so busy. And, between you and me, I'm hoping some of these folks just turn around and head right back where they came from instead of moving into the area." She frowned. "Is that mean?"

"I don't know if it is, but I share your sentiment. I'm starting to feel like the old guys who hang out on the bench downtown. I'm wishing for the good old days."

Sally laughed and pointed a finger at me, assuming a crotchety voice. "Get off my lawn you whippersnapper!"

I chuckled as she stood, shoving a frizzy lock of dirty blonde hair behind one ear. "Oh well. It will be what it will be, I guess. I'll see ya later, Joey. You take care now, 'kay?"

"I will. You too." As she buzzed herself into the examination area, I had a thought. "Hey, you don't happen to know anybody who Penney Sellers might have hacked off in particular, do you?"

Sally pulled the door open and held it, her gaze narrowing thoughtfully. "I know a few. There's the Johnstons out your way. That woman actually told Mr. Johnston he was too old to still have such a remote home and said he'd be doing his kids a favor by selling it before he kicked."

My eyes went wide. "Oh my gosh!"

"Yeah." Sally shook her head. "Then there's that author fella who lives out by himself, south of town." She made a squinty face. "Abels, I think. He's a real private kind of guy. She marched up to his door big as you please and he couldn't get rid of her. She told him he'd write better books if he stepped out of his safety zone." Sally arched an eyebrow as I shook my head. "She suggested he get an apartment in downtown Indianapolis and assured him she'd have no trouble at all selling his place."

"Jeezopete," I breathed.

"It's kind of a wonder he didn't just kill her on the spot and bury her in the woods. He does write murder mysteries after all."

"Thanks for the information, Sally."

She nodded. "Good luck finding the cat a home. I wish I could take her, but my boyfriend is deathly allergic to cats. Breaks out in hives as big as golf balls if he so much as looks at one."

I considered Sally's information while I waited for Hal. She'd given me a couple of possibilities, though Mr. Johnston, who was probably eighty-years-old, seemed like an unlikely suspect. Still, he could swing a big stick or a bat at the woman's head. So, we'd talk to him.

Harold Abels was a much better possibility. I'd met him once at a book signing in *Barker's Books* on Main Street. If I recalled correctly, he didn't seem to fit the description of the guy Penney Sellers had been arguing with, per Marge. Abels had been sitting down when I met him, but I remembered him as a small man and I was pretty sure he didn't have much hair. He was also almost painfully introverted. But I knew the deadliest currents sometimes ran beneath a placid surface.

Caught up in my thoughts, I almost missed Hal's return to the waiting room. Thank goodness, LaLee pulled me right out of my reverie by growling long and low as soon as she clapped eyes on him.

Hal the rat dumped me in front of my house with the kennel bouncing around down by my feet and skedaddled, with a murmured excuse I only half heard. I'm pretty sure it had something to do with scrubbing toilets.

Though I could have misheard that.

With a long-suffering sigh, I reached down and clasped the handles of the bouncing kennel, tugging it off the ground as it tipped violently from side to side. Some truly terrifying sounds emerged as I lifted. "Calm down, LaLee. You're going to scare the pibl."

The cat hissed to let me know what she thought about that.

"You might not care if you scare the dog but you will. Scared dogs bite. And she's got much bigger teeth than you do."

A soft growl was the only response I got.

I stopped at the door, my hand on the knob, and took a bracing breath. Caphy snorfled against the door on the other side, anxious for me to come inside.

When I didn't immediately open the door, the pibl barked unhappily. Her nails clicked on the hardwood floor as she ran to the window in the living room which overlooked the porch.

Her wide, smushy face appeared in the slobbered-up glass. She whined as she spotted me, her wide body shifting from side to side as she worked her muscular tail.

I hated to open the door and upend her world. But I had to do it. Maybe the two animals would surprise me.

Maybe they'd get along.

I pushed open the door, and Caphy lunged out, shoving her face toward the window of the kennel, her nose twitching with interest.

"Yowl! Hissssss!" A paw snapped through one of the small squares that made up the "window" and Caphy shot backward with a yelp just in time to avoid being slashed by the cat's claws.

My dog did an about-face and ran into the living room, diving behind the overstuffed leather recliner in front of the fireplace.

I carried the kennel inside and placed it on the tile in front of the door

Caphy didn't come to see me. She peeked at us from under the chair, her gaze locked like a laser on the kennel.

"Come here, Caphy. I'm sorry, girl."

I heard the soft thump of her tail on the rug and then nothing. She wasn't coming out from behind that recliner unless I pulled her out.

I bent down and looked at her underneath the chair. "It's okay, honey. The cat can't get you." All I saw was a pair of worried green eyes and a twitching nose on top of two fat paws.

I left the cat by the door and walked over to see my dog. Sitting down on the floor, I held out a hand and, after a final glance toward the demon in the carrier, she slumped over and lay down, her head on my lap.

I kissed the soft squishiness of her wide head. "It's only for a little while, girl. I promise."

Caphy whined, but her gaze never strayed from the carrier in the entranceway.

"She's kind of cranky, but I'm sure she's scared," I told my dog. I knew I was really trying to reassure myself as much as Caphy. She didn't understand the words, but my tone of voice was set to soothe, and she relaxed slightly underneath it.

The hair on her back smoothed down a titch.

My cell rang and I pulled it out of my purse, frowning down at the ID on the screen. Why would *Deer Hollow Realtors* be calling me?

Then I remembered giving Madge my number and answered. "Hello?"

"Joey Fulle?"

"Yes?'

"This is Madge down at *Deer Hollow Realtors*."

"Hey, Madge. Did you think of something else about Penney?"

"No. I mean. I didn't think of anything. I saw something."

"What did you see?"

"You remember you asked about the guy Penney was fighting with?"

I sat up straighter, excitement lifting my pulse. "I do."

"Well, he was just here. I saw him climbing out of his car at *Junior's*." *Junior's* was the local grocery store in the center of *Deer Hollow*. It was one of those small-town IGAs that are so prevalent in the Midwest. But people in the area called it *Junior's* after its owner, Junior Milliard. I stood up and Caphy dove back behind the chair again. "Is he still there?"

"No. He drove away a couple minutes ago."

I deflated, disappointed.

"But I snapped his picture. I'm sending it to you now."

My phone dinged as the photo arrived. I opened *Messages*, hitting the photo with my finger to enlarge it.

I sucked in a horrified gasp.

I was looking at Hal, shoving the door closed on his big, black Escalade.

CHAPTER SEVEN

I carried the kennel to my parents' old room and closed the door behind me. Unzipping the opening in the carrier, I walked away to fill a bowl with water in the master bath.

The cat didn't come out. In fact, she'd gone silent and very still. I could feel her staring at me through the opening, her gaze burning a hole right between my shoulder blades. I set the bowl of water close to the carrier. "I'll be back soon, LaLee, and I'll give you some yummy tuna for dinner." I crouched down and tried to peer at her through the open door of the kennel.

All I could see was the eerie glow of her eyes as they caught sunlight from the window. "I need to get you a litter box too, don't I?"

The glowing eyes didn't shift a millimeter. I barely suppressed a shudder. "You'll be comfy here. You can sleep on the bed as well as climb up on the window seat and look outside. You'll have fun exploring all the nooks and crannies." I stood up a moment later when the cat continued to stare at me, unresponsive and cold. The unpleasant critter was obviously judging me inadequate as a caregiver.

I felt bad leaving her, but I shook it off. It was normal for LaLee to be nervous in her new surroundings. The most important thing was to keep her safe and comfortable until I found her a place to live.

She didn't have to love me.

Though it would be nice if she could look at me without that expression of complete and utter disgust.

Sigh...

I stopped at the door and looked back. The kennel didn't even tremble.

Guilt ate at me. I wasn't sure if I was enclosing her in my parents' room because it was best for me or for her.

It was definitely best for Caphy. And I owed my dog that at least. So in the end, I shoved the guilt away as I tugged the door closed and Caphy and I headed out again.

We didn't get far. Hal was coming down my driveway as Caphy and I walked outside. He stopped the car in the circular drive and climbed out, catching a manically happy pit bull as she threw herself at him.

Did I imagine the accusing glance my dog threw me as Hal wrapped himself around her wriggling body? "Hey, beauty. What did you think of your new friend?"

"She's not a fan," I told Hal, walking over as he extricated himself from my dog and opened a back car door. "I realized as I was leaving that you'd need some supplies. So, I went back into town and grabbed cat food, litter, and a litter box."

All the mean thoughts I'd had about him leaving fled, and I found myself smiling. "You read my mind. I was just going to do that."

"Well, now you don't have to." Before I realized what he was going to do, he lowered his lips and touched mine in a soft, lingering kiss that curled my toes.

I closed my eyes and let pleasure swirl through me. He broke the kiss all too soon. "I'm sorry."

My eyes blinked open. He looked down at me, his face filled with misery.

"I only wanted to surprise you. I realize now how it looks and for that I'm sorry. I promise I'm *really* happy to be here with you."

My mind reeling over the quick change of subject, I could only nod. It felt as if my eyes were twice their normal size.

"You're still mad?"

I realized my silence felt like judgment and shook my head. "No. I might have overreacted." I touched his arm. "I just don't want you to feel compelled..."

He put a warm finger over my lips, stopping my attempt to save face. "You're not compelling me to do anything. I'm a big boy. I made this choice. I'm happy with it." He leaned back against the car, his arms filled with bags of cat stuff. "I'll still need to spend time in Indianapolis of course. I have active clients there and Cal depends on me."

"Of course." My stomach jittered happily. Excitement replacing the anger and fear that had been there.

"But most days I can make the trip back and forth in one day. It's only an hour and a half."

I nodded. "What about your apartment on Broad Ripple?"

"I'm holding onto it for the time being. If nothing else, we can put clients up there when extra protection is needed."

"A safe house on the canal?" I grinned. "I'm feeling very unsafe."

He laughed. "You don't need to be in danger to spend time there, you know. Just tell me when, and we can go take in some shows, do some shopping."

That sounded like a lot of fun. "It's a deal."

He sighed. "But right now, we have a murder to solve. After we get the cat settled, are you up for some sleuthing?"

"I thought you'd never ask. What did you have in mind?"

"I thought we'd talk to some of the business owners in town. Apparently, Ms. Sellers has been harassing a lot of them about selling. As unlikely as it seems, they all have to hit the suspect list."

Just like that, I remembered that he had a spot on that list. I did a mental head slap. I couldn't believe I'd forgotten what Madge had told me not fifteen minutes earlier. That was the effect the man in front of me had on my brain. "Hold on. I need to talk to you about something before we leave."

He eyed me carefully. "Sure. What's up?"

"I went to speak to Madge over at *Deer Hollow Realtors.*"

"I know. I saw you there, remember?"

"Yeah. By the way, why were you there?"

His frown was fleeting, quickly dissipating as he shrugged. "I'm guessing the same thing you were there for. I wanted to find out if her partner knew of anybody who'd threatened Penny Sellers, or if there was anyone she'd recently had a problem with."

I stared at him a long moment. He was either being coy or... "You mean besides you?"

Surprise flickered across his features. "Me?" He seemed genuinely confused for a beat. Then his expression cleared. "Ah, you mean because I argued with her that day..." He nodded. "I didn't realize her partner was there."

"Okay. That's not making me feel any better."

He sighed. "It was nothing. I found out Penney had been talking to Deb at the bank about the value of my property. Specifically if I subdivided the acreage. I didn't appreciate it and I told her so."

I wouldn't have appreciated that either. "What did she say?"

"You met her right?"

I nodded, wincing.

"She reacted about like you'd expect her to. She pretended

not to know what I was talking about and then got belliger-
ent. She seemed to think that because homes and properties
were her business, everything about everybody else's homes
and properties was also her business." Hal shook his head.

I chewed the inside of my lip, not wanting to ask him the
next question but knowing I needed to. He caught my
expression and saved me from my self.

"Look, I won't say the woman didn't make me really mad.
She did. I won't even deny the brief urge to flick her really
hard on the end of her nose with my finger. But kill her? No.
She wasn't worth the prison time."

"Do you have an alibi for the time she was killed?"

He raised both eyebrows. "You saw me at my cabin."

"I did. But it would have only taken you ten minutes to
bop on over here, clock her on the head, and bop
back home."

His lips twitched. "Bop and clock, huh?"

I shrugged.

"You don't really believe I did that, right? Because, if I
thought you believed that, we would have bigger problems
than me keeping that cabin a secret for a couple of months."

I frowned, shrugging. "Of course, I don't believe it. But
before we can move forward, you need to take yourself out of
the running."

He expelled a long breath of air. "The electrician actually
stopped by before you came. He and I discussed the option
of security floodlights on the exterior of the place. He was
probably there an hour. Then you and Caphy came. And after
you left I called Cal and we went over one of our cases
together."

"Being on the phone isn't a good alibi," I said, frowning.
"You could have taken the cell phone with you to my house."

He nodded. "That's true. But I was doing Facetime with
my brother the entire time. Cal's a pretty good PI. He would

probably have noticed if I clocked Penney Sellers over the head while I was talking to him about round the clock surveillance options for a client."

I fought the smile trying to form on my lips. "I'm just making sure. Arno's going to go down the same path I have, and he'll ask for an alibi."

"Already has. He contacted both the electrician and Cal right away." Hal winced. "Big brother wants to come down here and help me clear my name."

I felt my eyes go round. The women of *Deer Hollow* would never survive a dual invasion of Amity brothers. The ground would tremble under all that hotness. "Is Felicity coming?" Despite my concern for Hal, I couldn't keep the excitement out of my voice.

"Neither one of them is coming. I told him I'm just fine and that you and I were on the case."

"Oh." Disappointment fought pride. "I guess that would be too many cooks in this stew."

"Way too many," Hal agreed. "Now, how about you and I head into town and talk to some potential suspects?"

"Sounds like a plan."

CHAPTER EIGHT

Since it was close to lunchtime and I'd lost out on my slice of banana cream pie the night before when I'd stormed out of the cabin, I opted to start with *Sonny's Diner*.

Erm...I mean. Given its importance to the community, the diner seemed like a very important first step in our investigation.

Better?

Situated in the center of *Deer Hollow*'s main street, *Sonny's Diner* was the heartbeat of the tiny town. People came to *Sonny's* from miles around to get great food served in an atmosphere where homey and comfortable fought tooth and nail with dumpy and sketchy for top billing.

Main street is really *Deer Hollow*'s *only* street. The angry outbursts of asphalt and gravel protruding from either side were too short and uneven to be called roads, and the mismatched array of lumps hunkered down along those outbursts represented the town's unassuming and slightly off-putting array of businesses and homes.

To near universal community relief, the restaurant was no longer owned by Sonny, whose real name had been Matthew

Earl. He'd generally been a terrible person. A self-centered only child whose doting mother had called him Sonny for no explicable reason.

Sonny's daughter Max was the current owner of the humble little diner, which squatted under a massive sign promising the best banana cream pie in the state. That was no lie.

Now if the sign had promised modern décor and booths whose torn plastic seats didn't scratch your behind...that would have been not just a lie but a dang lie.

A cheerful bell jangled when I opened the door, and a handful of locals turned away from their chicken and noodles with mashed potatoes to check me out. Their gazes swept quickly over me and got caught on Hal, tightening with distrust for a moment, before returning to the delicious, carb-filled glops on their yellowed plastic plates.

My nose twitched with delight under the scent of rich chicken broth and buttery mashed potatoes.

"What smells so good?" Hal asked, his eyes alight.

"The best chicken and noodles you'll ever taste," I told him, grinning from ear to ear. I pointed to a back booth when Max looked up from the order she was taking at the long, chipped linoleum counter. She caught my message and nodded.

I carefully scooted into the least torn side of the booth and sat there vibrating with excitement.

Hal eyed me. "You okay?"

"Great!" I told him in an over-enthusiastic tone.

He flinched. "How much coffee have you had today?"

"Only two cups. Maybe three." I squinted my eyes in thought. "Definitely no more than four. Why?"

"Because you're vibrating like a mouse on a washer in spin cycle."

I laughed gaily. "It's not the coffee. I'm excited about lunch."

He eyed me again. "You do love your vittles."

"Is that a country bumpkin reference?"

"Not at all. I was just trying to fit in."

"Then it was an epic fail. Nobody around here says vittles."

The bell jangled again, and we looked up to find a heavy-set elderly man wearing a plaid flannel coat and sporting a toothpick in his teeth. He was headed out, but before he left, he lifted a hand to Max. "Great vittles, Max!"

Jeezopete!

I fought the urge to stick my tongue out at Hal when he gave me a smug grin. "Nobody under ninety says that anyway."

His chuckle made me flush with embarrassment.

"Hey, kids," Max said, dropping menus in front of us.

Smiling up at the woman with the ratty tangle of yellow-white hair piled on top of her head, I gave the curled-plastic-covered list of goodies a cursory glance and handed it back. "I know what I want."

Max was already writing on her pad. "Chicken and noodles and creampie." She made the word "pie" sound like waa with a p.

I grinned my response.

"Green beans for cover?" she asked.

I nodded.

Max looked at Hal. He shook his head. "Make that two of everything. Even the cover beans, though I have no idea what that means."

Max walked away while writing in her pad.

"This meal is pure decadent delight," I explained to Hal. "Carb on carb crime. The green beans give it respectability. Sort of."

Hal chuckled. "Works for me."

Less than five minutes later, Max was back, placing two oversized bowls filled with a mound of mashed potatoes covered by a glistening gravy filled with dense, chewy noodles and big chunks of chicken. She slid the slices of pie onto the front of the table and eyed the bounty. "Can I get you two anything else?"

"A bib?" Hal asked, picking up his fork. "I'm not sure what kind of mental condition I'll be in when I finish all this. I might be in a carb coma."

Max gave him a crooked smile. "It won't be anything we haven't seen before."

I took a bite, moaning softly as my teeth sank into a dense, chewy noodle. "Delicious," I told Max. "Actually, we were wondering if you could tell us about your experience with Penney Sellers."

Max's grin died an immediate death, replaced by a look of pure disgust. "I didn't kill her," she said. "But Lord help me, I did consider it."

Hal nodded in agreement, chewing.

"She tried to get you to sell Sonny's?"

"Worse. Would you believe she wanted to tear the whole building down and put in some kind of vegetarian grill or something?"

"What kind of vegetables would you even grill? I asked.

Max shrugged. "She mentioned squash steaks or some such nonsense. I told her I prefer my squash whipped into a casserole or pie with lots of lard and sugar." Max's grin made a quick, temporary return. "I thought she was going to swallow her tongue on that one."

I looked at Hal. "I'm sensing a theme here."

"Yeah." He swiped his napkin over his lips and looked down at his empty bowl, a look of perplexity on his face. "Did you eat my food?" he asked me.

I snorted out a laugh. He looked at Max, and she threw up her hands. "Wasn't me. You want more?"

Though he looked really unhappy about it, he shook his head. "I'd better not. This place is going to be death to my waistline."

"Why thank you," Max said.

Hal leaned toward Max, lowering his voice. "She came at me about the cabin I just bought outside of town. She wanted me to sell it to her so she could tear it down and subdivide the land."

Max glanced my way.

Swallowing a bite, I explained. "Dev's place."

"Ah..." Max said, nodding. "Nice property. I hate to say it, but that woman didn't understand *Deer Hollow*'s charm. She sang the same song everywhere she went. Tear stuff down and start over. I think she had in mind to build someplace more hip."

"It would take a pretty big bankroll to buy up a whole town, tear it down and rebuild," Hal said.

I agreed. "Her place was nice, but I didn't get the feeling she had *that* kind of money."

"If she did, that partner of hers would know."

"What do you know about them?" Hal asked Max.

"Not much. I know they came from Indianapolis. Had an office in the Broad Ripple area, I heard. But I don't think they were there for very long either."

"Lots of old buildings, clubs, and restaurants on Broad Ripple," I told them. "If she tried the same thing there..."

"She'd have been thrown out on her keister," Max said on a nod. "Her way didn't make her many friends."

"No," Hal said, pushing his empty bowl aside. "In fact, I'm wondering if it didn't make her an enemy who was mad enough to follow her down here."

Max shrugged and then slid her gaze back to me. "I'm guessing she tried to get her hands on your place too?"

"She did. I closed the door in her face." I dropped my fork into my empty bowl. "Unfortunately, she snuck back later and got her head bashed in at my pond."

"Really?" Max's eyes went wide. "I'd heard she was killed, but I didn't realize it was at your place." Her expression turned soft. "Oh, honey. I'm sorry."

I nodded. "That's why Hal and I are asking so many questions. We're trying to find out why she was there and who killed her."

"And you don't think Arno will figure it out?" The censure was gentle. Max had known the deputy sheriff since he was in diapers, but she also knew how stubborn and set in his ways he could be.

"He will," I said as she picked up my and Hal's empty bowls. "But I'm sure he'd appreciate our help." My grin felt kind of strained.

She barked out a laugh. "I wouldn't count on that. Well, if I was gonna look at people who might want to bash that horrible woman over the head and dump her in your pond, I'd start with old Devon. You haven't heard from him, have you?"

I shook my head. "Not for over a month. He knows if he comes back, Arno's gonna want to talk to him about the last time he showed up."

Max nodded. "Well, whatever you want to say about that guy, he's always been very protective of you, honey. If he thought Penney Sellers was a danger to you or your inheritance, he just might take things into his own hands."

I nodded, knowing she was right. "I don't disagree. It's just that I don't know where he is."

Max glanced at Hal. "You say you bought his place? You've spoken to him?"

Hal shook his head. "I dealt with a lawyer here in town to buy the property. George Shulz."

Max made a face. "I know George." The way she said it, I figured she didn't like him much. I'd never met the man.

She patted me on the shoulder. "I'll get you two clean forks. Would you like coffee to go with that pie?"

"Sounds great," I told her. Hal nodded, giving her a grateful smile.

We climbed into Hal's Escalade, our bellies so full we groaned as we moved. "I might need a nap," Hal said. "I don't think I've ever been this full before."

"Stick with me," I said, grinning. "Comfort food is kind of my thing."

"Oh, I intend to," he agreed, turning the key. The engine started with a rumble, and he glanced my way. "Who do you want to talk to first?"

I flushed with pleasure from his words, looking away with embarrassment. "When I was waiting for you at the hospital, I was talking to a friend of mine there. She's a nurse. She told me Penney Sellers harassed that mystery writer outside town."

"Scott Abels?" Hal asked, frowning. "Isn't he a recluse?"

"Pretty much," I agreed. "Sally said Penney Sellers was brutal to him. It wouldn't hurt to find out if he has an alibi."

He nodded. "He lives south of town, right?"

I nodded. "His road's on the right, just after *Mitzner's*."

Mitzner's Landscaping was the largest greenhouse and landscaping store and service within sixty miles of *Deer Hollow*. Hal and I had bumped up against the owner, Buck Mitzner, the last time I'd found a dead body. Buck was everybody's idea of a jerk and, if Penney Sellers had spoken to him, he'd definitely be on my short list for her killer. "I wonder if Buck had the pleasure of meeting our Ms. Sellers?"

Hal shook his head. "Mitzner's wasn't in that journal you found."

My eyes went wide. "I'd forgotten about the journal. You've been going over it?"

He nodded. "Cal and I talked about it this morning. He thinks there's a good chance we could be looking at title fraud."

I frowned. "Title fraud? Why does he think that?"

"Because of the victim's unusual interest in the bank assessment of these properties..."

"But isn't that an important piece of data for a Realtor?" I interrupted.

"Market value is important. But bank value isn't necessarily something a realtor considers until the appraisal stage." He slanted me a look as he hit the highway and picked up speed. "But if you want to take out loans on properties for which you'd stolen the title, the bank value is important."

"Ah," I said, nodding. I thought about the pages in the journal. "You know, that theory clarifies that second column of numbers we couldn't figure out."

"If you assume that's the amount of money the thief can wring from a stolen title, it does, yes."

My eyes went wide. "Hal, she had my house on that list."

"No worries. Cal and I are working on that."

"How?"

"He knows a guy who sells title insurance. He'll get you a partner deal."

"Thanks." I relaxed. Until I realized everybody else in *Deer Hollow* was in trouble. "What about Max, and the rest?"

"Hopefully Miss Sellers was working alone and the threat is gone now that she is. But Cal and I are going to run security checks on everybody in her journal. If anybody's been exposed, we'll make sure they're protected."

My chest tightened with emotion, and tears filled my eyes. "You guys are pretty special. You know that?"

He reached over and grabbed my hand, giving it a warm squeeze. "We didn't really have a choice. Felly threatened to smack him upside the head with her biggest purse if we didn't help you."

I laughed. "I don't even think you're lying about that."

Scott Abels' place was set way back from the road, at the end of a long, winding driveway with "No Trespassing" signs peppered along its length. I fully expected a gated entrance when we reached the end of the drive, but there was no gate.

The house was a colonial style, white clapboard with black shutters and a covered porch that ran the width of the house.

The porch was sans furniture or any other softening items. The landscaping was minimal, consisting mainly of boxy shrubs and a couple of small trees. A sea of grass spread around the house, about ten acres of it, if I had to guess, and ended at a distant line of mature trees that ringed it like a fence and ran all the way to the road.

The land had likely once been farmland, and it was stark. No other homes were visible around Abels' house. The place felt remote and was almost uncomfortably quiet.

We climbed out of the Escalade and headed up the sidewalk to the front door. It was painted black like the shutters and had no glass or any adornment, such as a door knocker.

There wasn't even a doorbell.

Clearly, Scott Abels didn't encourage company. A fact that

was underscored by the mat in front of the door, which read, "Go away. This is not a joke."

I pointed to it, and Hal shook his head, knocking firmly on the door. We looked around, baked in silence, as his knock was apparently ignored.

Five knocks later, the door finally opened to show us a small man with a balding head and irritation writ-large across his round face. Scott Abels looked exactly as I remembered him. "I'm assuming you didn't see all the *No Trespassing* signs?"

Hal held out his PI's license. "We're sorry to bother you, Mr. Abels."

The man took the license and examined it carefully, then handed it back and started to close the door. "You and I have no business together, Mr. Amity."

Hal reached out and grasped the edge of the door, stopping it. "This will only take a moment, sir. I promise."

Abels expelled a long-suffering sigh. "I'll give you that minute and nothing more. Go."

"It's our understanding that Realtor Penney Sellers visited you recently."

His expression was filled with repugnance. "Horrid woman."

"Were you aware she'd been killed?" Hal asked.

Abels' expression didn't change. "There is a God, apparently."

"You don't seem surprised," I put in.

He turned to me, his upper lip curling. "Who are you?"

I offered him my hand and a smile. "I'm Joey Fulle. And the unfortunate hostess of Miss Seller's dead body."

His eyes went wide. "I know your story. About your parents."

I barely kept from wincing. "It wasn't exactly a secret."

"Not at all. Fascinating case. I wonder if you'd be willing to sit down with me sometime. I'd love to get your perspective on what happened. It would make a riveting murder mystery."

Hal nudged my arm ever so slightly. He wanted me to play along.

I forced myself to respond. "Maybe we could work something out, Mr. Abels…"

"Please, call me Scott. Would you like to come inside?"

Hal must have seen me stiffen with dread. I hadn't come out there anticipating dredging up my parents' death with a man who wanted to turn it into a sensational account for one of his books.

"No, thank you, Mr. Abels," Hal said. "We have another appointment. We just wanted to find out if you had any idea who might have killed Ms. Sellers."

"Anybody who'd spent five minutes with her," the man ground out through a clenched jaw. "She was horrible. And I'm pretty sure she had illegal intentions."

"Why do you say that?" I asked.

"Because after she left, she tried to find out about my finances. Fortunately, since I'm trying to refinance right now, I happened to be speaking with Doris at the bank and she told me the woman had been sniffing around. Apparently, she'd also run a credit check on me. Needless to say my antennas were engaged. If that horrible woman hadn't been killed, I'd have been confronting her about it in the near future."

"How did she do that?" Hal asked. "She would have needed your permission unless you initiated business with her."

"I understand she represented herself as my realtor. I have no idea how she did it. Only that she did."

"She must have forged your signature," Hal said.

Abels shrugged. "I wouldn't have put it past her."

"I have to ask, sir. Where were you yesterday between four and six PM?"

Abels stared at Hal for a long moment and then shook his head. "I was here. As I always am, working."

"Can anyone verify that, sir?"

"No. And let me save you the speculation. I know a hundred ways to kill somebody. I've crafted a thousand alibis and definitely had reason to murder that horrible woman. But hurt feelings aren't a strong motive for killing someone. Despite the fact that it would have been a pleasure to remove her from existence."

"So you're telling us you could have killed her?" Hal asked carefully.

"I could have, sure. But I didn't. And if you want to pin it on me, you're going to have to get really creative to place me at the scene. Your minute's up, Mr. Amity." He started to close the door and then stopped, glancing at me. "I look forward to talking to you about your parents, Miss Fulle."

"Yeah, when pigs fly," I murmured to the closed door.

CHAPTER NINE

"What did you think of that?" Hal asked me.

"I think Abels would have to be pretty stupid to tout his qualifications for murder if he did it."

Hal nodded. "My thoughts exactly. But Arno's not going to take him off the list of suspects unless he can prove he wasn't there when she was killed."

I shivered, rubbing my arms. "This is all so sad. That woman hurt everyone she touched. How terrible it must be to live your life that way."

Hal turned down my driveway. "She certainly paid a price for it." He stopped the SUV in front of my house. "Why don't you let me stay with you. I'd feel better if you weren't alone." When I hesitated, he pressed his case. "I need to call Cal and work some more on that case. I'll stay out of your way. You won't even know I'm here."

He'd been looking at me as if I were a delicate piece of china ever since I'd told him I wanted to come home. I couldn't explain my need to be home with Caphy and to check on my new tenant. Talking to Scott Abels had depressed me. And I was having trouble shaking it off.

I suspected it had something to do with his cavalier treatment of my parents' death, but I didn't want to tell Hal that. I wasn't up to having that conversation again.

I shook my head. I wasn't even sure why I was digging my heels in, but deep down I knew it probably still had something to do with the cabin thing.

I'd pretty much forgiven him for not telling me he was buying the place. But that didn't mean I was going to go right back to normal with him. I needed time to soothe my hurt feelings and come to an acceptance of our new normal. "I'll be fine. I have Caphy and the attack cat. Nobody's going to come near me with LaLee here."

"Including me," he grumbled. He probably didn't even realize he was rubbing his furrowed chin. Feeling a quick jolt of tenderness for him, I leaned in and pressed my lips against his. Heat flared between us immediately, and I nearly forgot why it wasn't a good idea for him to come inside. I reluctantly broke the kiss a minute later, and climbed out of his car. "Thanks for going with me today."

He nodded. "If you hear or see anything tonight that makes you uncomfortable, call me. I don't care what time it is. I'll be up late anyway doing some research for a case."

"I will."

"Promise?"

"Girl Scout's honor and all that."

"I'm pretty sure you were never a girl scout."

I grinned. "You don't know that."

He shook his head and, with a final heated look in my direction, pulled away and headed out to *Goat's Hollow Road*. I watched him turn left, so I was pretty sure he was heading for the cabin, and then went to let my wildly barking dog out to pee.

I left Caphy outside while I went into the kitchen and filled a bowl with unappetizing-looking dry cat food for my foster fur baby. After a second's thought, I dug a can of tuna out of the cabinet and added some of that to the dry food in the bowl.

I blenched at the fishy smell of the concoction but figured the cat would probably love it.

Caphy was whining at the door by the time I started upstairs. I briefly considered leaving her out there until I'd fed the cat, but decided that wouldn't be fair. I'd promised myself I wouldn't let having LaLee in the house totally disrupt Caphy's life. A little disruption was bound to happen, but I needed to keep it to a minimum.

With that resolution firmly in mind, I let Caphy in and took her into the kitchen, pulling one of her favorite green chews out of the cabinet and giving it to her before heading upstairs.

The cat didn't attack when I cracked the bedroom door. I'll admit I was braced for it and ready to slam the door closed if a cat-shaped projectile flew at my face when I opened it.

I stood just inside the closed door and looked around, calling LaLee in a voice that was hopefully soft enough not to startle.

Nothing.

"I brought you food, girl." I walked over to the kennel, realizing halfway there that I was walking on my tiptoes, and forced myself to stop. "This is silly. Come out now and get this food I so thoughtfully provided you."

Nothing.

I set the food down on the floor next to the water dish and then took the water bowl into the bathroom to refresh it. While waiting for the bowl to fill, I saw a tiny movement out of the corner of my eye. Turning toward the movement, I found LaLee sitting upright, like something from an Egyptian tomb, in the center of the shower. Her distrustful blue gaze locked on me, and her slender form went very still. "Hey, girl."

The gaze didn't soften or waver. I got the impression she was poised to attack if she deemed it necessary. It was my goal to *not* make her feel like it was necessary. I slowly reached out and turned off the water. "I'll just leave this food and water out here. You can have some when you're ready. Okay?" I felt kind of silly talking to the cat, especially since she was regarding me with such disdain.

Clearly, she thought I was an idiot, displaying disgust in every line of her perfect feline form.

"Cats," I murmured. "So judgmental."

I eased slowly back out of the bathroom and left the water next to the food. After checking the litter box to make sure it was clean, I left the room and the cat, hoping she'd begin to realize I meant her no harm.

I went downstairs and felt myself at a loss. Glancing around my kitchen, I thought about fixing something to eat. But my lunch still sat heavy on my belly. I'd be eating just because I was bored.

Never a good thing.

I thought about the murder mystery waiting for me on my bedside table, but the idea of settling in to read just didn't appeal.

Then I thought about the other names my friend Sally Winthrop had given me and wondered if I should talk to the Johnstons. I was saved from making a decision by the ringing of my phone.

It was Arno. "Saved by the bell," I told him when I answered.

"What bell?"

I smiled. He was so literal. "Nothing. What's up? Do you have cause of death?"

"I do. I shouldn't be sharing it with you, but I thought

you had a right to know, given that Ms. Sellers was killed on your property."

"Okay," I said in an impatient voice. "I'm waiting."

He hesitated another beat. I couldn't help feeling like he was doing it just to tweak me. Then he said something that turned my belly to ice. "Penney Sellers was strangled and drowned."

"Strangled and drowned? How's that possible?"

"My guess is whoever strangled her held her underwater while they did it."

I shuddered. "Horrible."

"Yeah. It speaks of real rage."

"From what I've learned talking to people, Penney Sellers inspired a lot of that."

His silence was sufficient warning of my faux pas.

"I mean, you know, just talking to people randomly on the street."

"You've been investigating this?"

"Only a little. Besides, Hal said you asked him to help."

"I asked for him to do some legwork, yes. But I didn't ask him to invite you along. You realize you're sniffing out a killer, right?"

"Of course. I'm not in any danger..."

"Yes. You are. And you need to stop. I asked Amity for help because he's a professional. He can take care of himself."

Anger caused my pulse to spike. "Because he's a big strong man and I'm just a puny, helpless woman?"

"Something like that."

I made a sound of outrage and I could almost hear him smiling. "Look, Joey. I know you're anything but helpless, but whoever killed this woman wasn't just going after *her*. They might have been sending you a message too."

"What are you talking about?"

"We found the murder weapon. It was lying in some tall grass alongside the pond."

"Great. Can you get DNA from it?"

His bristling came across the line like an electric shock. "I *am* trained for this, you know."

I bit back a sigh. "Sorry. I just got excited."

"Well, don't be. Because I think the weapon was left there on purpose. To implicate you."

The ice ball in my belly grew from golf ball sized to softball sized. "Why do you say that?"

"Because Penney Sellers was strangled with Caphy's leash."

All thoughts of hunkering down at home were blown away by Arno's revelation. I suddenly had an all-consuming need to take action. It had just turned personal, and I knew I had to find out who was trying to set me up for Penney Seller's murder.

I disconnected with Arno and dialed Hal.

It rang several times before I gave up. It wasn't unusual, when Hal was elbows deep in a case, for him to miss a call or take a while to get back to me. I figured he and his brother were probably on the phone together working on that case he'd mentioned earlier.

I paced my kitchen, feeling antsy. Caphy lay on the floor in front of the door and rolled her eyes back and forth, watching me pace.

Every once in a while, her muscular tail snapped once against the floor in solidarity. I considered stopping by Hal's cabin to see if he wanted to go with me. But I didn't want to interrupt his work.

Besides, Arno's comments about me being unsuited for sniffing out a killer had stung.

Sure, he was right. I wasn't trained for taking down bad guys like he and Hal were. But I wasn't planning on going anywhere near a killer.

I just wanted to talk to a couple of octogenarians about a pushy realtor.

And I *would* have backup. I planned on taking Caphy with me.

Finally, I couldn't take it anymore. "Come on, girl."

I grabbed Caphy's leash off the hook on the wall and started to walk out of the kitchen. A disturbing thought popped into my head as Arno's words finally sank all the way in. I skidded to a stop, my gaze sliding toward the hooks. The ball of ice in my belly grew another inch.

Panic set in. Followed immediately by a deep sense of violation.

Someone had to have been inside my house to get hold of one of the leashes.

I tried to remember where my other leash had been the last time I'd seen it. I usually took one of them with us when Caphy and I took our walks in the woods, just in case I needed to keep her from chasing squirrels or, more recently, from disrupting the occasional dead body.

We'd walked the morning before. In my mind's eye, I remembered sliding the leash over its customary hook before slipping off my sneakers. I couldn't remember if the second leash had been hanging there. In fact, I couldn't remember the last time I'd seen it.

My gaze slid to the dingy old pair of sneaks I sometimes wore when we walked in the woods and found them sitting in the rubber tray that I used to keep the floor clean.

I frowned.

One sneaker was cattywampus, its scuffed and dirty toe

resting on the other shoe. Had I thrown them into the tray that way? I generally placed them carefully, allowing a smidge of self-diagnosed OCD to guide my movements.

With a horrified start, I realized someone had been inside my house.

My first thought was Uncle Devon. Maybe he *had* returned. Despite the fact that I'd taken his key away from him, he always seemed able to get inside the house.

But I dismissed the thought as quickly as it came.

For all his faults, Max had been right on with her assessment of what motivated him. He was just about as far from a saint as anyone could be, but he'd never deliberately harm me.

I believed that with all my heart.

And he certainly wouldn't try to point suspicion for a murder in my direction.

Rubbing my arms as gooseflesh popped along my skin, I reached down and scratched the wide spot between my Pitbull's ears. "Come on, girl. We need to find out who's targeting us before this turns ugly."

She whined softly as if my words bothered her, but she was more likely reading my nervousness. She was exceptionally good at that. And when I pulled the front door open, Caphy bounced happily outside, bounding toward my little car as if she hadn't a care in the world.

CHAPTER TEN

The Johnstons lived five minutes farther from town than I did, on *Baileyville Road. Baileyville* was a heavily wooded road that wound around *Deer County State Park* and dead-ended right after their rustic home. The house reminded me of an upscale cabin, with wrap-around porches and, at the center of the sprawling ranch, an enormous peak filled with glass that looked out over the stunning vista of rocky ridges, a rich umbrella of trees, and, in the distance, the sparkling ribbon of the river winding through the deep cut of the rocky landscape.

I debated leaving Caphy in the car, afraid she'd jump up on the couple, who were in their late seventies, early eighties, and might not have the strength to fend her off. But in the end, I opted for keeping her on a short leash and bringing her with.

Arno's words, however they might have annoyed me, still rang in my ears. Realizing the killer might very well have been inside my home didn't make me feel any safer.

Caphy peed several times on the short walk toward the glossy wood door made of rustic pine. When I tugged on her leash to get her going, she happily bounded forward, a big smile on her wide face. She loved nothing more than an adventure, and I could only guess that the woods where the Johnstons lived was rife with the scents of a variety of wild critters.

The pibl was in canine heaven.

The doorbell rang out in bell-like tones through the big house. Caphy bounced excitedly around the porch as footsteps started toward us, and I gave her leash a tug to settle her.

My pitty dutifully stilled, standing next to me with her gaze locked on the door, vibrating. She tilted her head when the lock was turned, and the door started to open.

I found myself looking into the softly pretty face of Belle Johnston. She looked much the way I remembered her, but younger than I'd thought. I wondered how much of my perception of the couple was colored by the fact that I'd been so young at the time.

Belle skimmed my dog a quick look and then glanced my way, her eyes lighting with pleasure. "Joey Fulle. How are you?"

I returned the smile she gave me. "I'm just wonderful, Mrs. Johnston. How about yourself?"

She nodded briskly. "Life is beautiful. Come inside, dear. I think I've got some freshly baked cookies left."

My mouth watered at the suggestion. So much for still being full from lunch.

"Would you like coffee? Tea? Or maybe a big glass of milk?" Her expression was friendly and somehow familiar. I had a feeling she was remembering me as I'd been when I was eight years old, and she used to bring platters of homemade peanut butter cookies to the Auction house when Mr. Johnston came to buy equipment.

She led me through the open, brightly rustic great room. I

marveled at the floor-to-ceiling fireplace of rock, enjoying the homey crackle of a vibrant fire.

The room was cheerful under the effects of the sunlight pouring through the wall of glass, and filled with the slightly smoky scent of the burning wood. An elegant baby grand piano claimed a spot in front of the impressive window.

"I'd love some milk. I don't dare drink anything with caffeine in it this late in the day." I glanced around the big, warm room. "Is Mr. Johnston around?"

"I'm afraid not. He had some errands to run in town. He'll be so sorry he missed you.

I followed her into a well-lit, oversized kitchen, and she motioned toward the table. "Have a seat, dear."

Caphy danced impatiently as I sat, and Belle bent to scratch her beneath her fleshy chin. "Hello, there beautiful. How are you today?"

Caphy's tongue swept out and bathed Mrs. Johnston's thin wrist. The old woman chuckled. "Miss Caphy, you are such a sweet baby." She looked at me. "Is it all right if I give her a cookie?"

I nodded. "She'd like that. As long as there's no chocolate in it."

Belle Johnston nodded, lifting a finger in my direction. "Thank you for reminding me. I'd almost forgotten about that. It's been so long since the Mr. and I had a fur baby."

I remembered a fat black Lab lumbering around the auction lot with Mr. Johnston. "Peanuts, right? She was a nice dog."

Belle's face filled with sweet remembrance. "Best dog we ever had. Unfortunately, we can't keep them as long as we'd like."

I sat at Belle's shiny round wood table. It was formed from golden oak that matched the cabinets in the bright kitchen. "Have you ever considered getting another dog?" I asked.

She shook her head. "A thousand times. But we're too old now. It wouldn't be fair to the dog."

How sad for them. "You could always make arrangements for family to take the dog if you..." I trailed off, realizing I should have kept my mouth shut. "If you should find yourself unable to care for it anymore." *Way to go, Joey,* I chastised myself.

Belle took pity on me and smiled. "That is a thought, dear." She poured me a tall glass of milk and set a plate filled with peanut butter cookies on the table. "No chocolate in these," she said as she selected one from the plate and broke off a chunk. "Sit, girl."

Caphy's butt hit the ground so fast it smacked loudly against the tile.

Belle laughed. "Good, girl." She offered the bite to Caphy, and my dog gently tugged it from her fingers.

"She's very food motivated," I explained as I stuffed a cookie into my mouth.

"It seems she's not the only one," Belle said on a chuckle.

Heat filled my face. As soon as I'd swallowed, I nodded. "I didn't realize how hungry I was until I saw these. I still remember you bringing them to the Auction when I was a kid."

"You do? Oh my. That was such a long time ago." She shook her head, breaking off another piece of the cookie and offering it to Caphy.

My dog was putty in her hands, her gaze locked on the cookie and her body rigid with anticipation.

I watched Mrs. Johnston feed Caphy the rest of the cookie and then ventured into the reason I'd come. "I'm sure you heard about the real estate agent who was killed?"

Belle nodded. She allowed Caphy to lick the crumbs off

her fingers and then straightened with a soft groan. She lifted her gaze to me, her blue eyes widening. "Oh. I just realized. She was killed on your property, wasn't she?"

"Unfortunately, yes."

Shaking her head, Belle went to wash her hands. She filled a metal teapot, settling it onto the center burner of her commercial-sized gas stove.

I totally lusted after that stove. Someday, I told myself, I'd get one of those. When I had enough people in my life to cook for.

That thought made me sad, so I shoved it away.

Belle glanced at me as she turned the fire up under the pot. "Terrible thing. I didn't care for her at all, of course. Thought she was very pushy." She frowned, tucking an errant gray-blonde curl behind one ear. "It's unkind to speak ill of the dead."

"I'm afraid there's a lot of that going on where Penney Sellers is concerned. I met her myself, and I'd have to agree with your assessment. In fact, her being on my property when she died is proof of it. I'd rejected her offer just a couple of hours earlier. If she was back, it was because she was ignoring that rejection."

"Edward told me she was murdered."

Edward was Mr. Johnston, Belle's husband. "That's the consensus, yes."

"How awful." Belle leaned against the counter and hugged herself, shuddering slightly. "Still, I can't imagine..." She slid a concerned gaze my way. "Did you find her?"

"Actually, Caphy found her. I just verified the finding." My grimace at the memory was unintentional, but it was honest.

"This isn't the first time for you, is it, dear?"

"No." I settled the rest of my cookie onto the plate. I'd lost my appetite. "But it darn sure better be the last, or I'm going to put a fence around my whole property, with a sign that says, *No Murders Allowed*."

Belle chuckled. "Well, I'm glad to see you've kept your sense of humor."

Little did she know I wasn't joking. Not about the fence part anyway. The influx of new people to *Deer Hollow* was becoming a deadly nuisance. "Can you tell me about her visit here?"

The teapot whistled. Belle pulled it off the burner and reached to an open shelf for a teacup. She lifted a brow to me. "Are you sure you won't have some?"

"No. But thank you. I'm good with the milk." I watched her fix her tea, adding honey to it and just a few drops of cream. It was the way my mom had always liked to drink her tea. That thought made my heart twist painfully. I couldn't help wondering if her loss would ever get easier.

When Belle had settled herself across from me, reaching for one of her own cookies, I decided to give her a little nudge.

"When Ms. Sellers was here, did you speak to her? Or was it Edward?"

"It was Edward. I was at the grocery, unfortunately. If I'd been here, I'd have given her a piece of my mind."

"What happened?"

Belle nibbled the edge of her cookie, her brows pinching together above it. "She waltzed right up to our door and all but demanded we sell the place."

If I hadn't met the pushy realtor, I'd have believed Belle was exaggerating. But since I had, I thought that probably came pretty close to the truth. "She wanted to list it herself?"

Belle shrugged. "I assume. To tell you the truth, the discussion never got that far. Edward told her very politely that we weren't interested in selling."

"Then what happened?"

"It was as if she didn't even hear him. She shoved one of her cards at him and proceeded to say that we were doing our heirs a disservice by sitting on the house. That we were obviously too old to care for such a large house and property and that our heirs would much rather receive the money from the sale of the house than be saddled with all of this to manage and dispose of." Tears filled her eyes, and I wanted to hit Penney Sellers over the head again because of it.

The Johnstons were kind people who only wanted their privacy and to be left alone to enjoy the little piece of heaven they'd worked hard all their lives to create.

Penney Sellers had been a monster.

"I'm so sorry you had to endure that."

She sniffled, nodding. "Thank you, dear. But you have nothing to apologize for. That woman certainly does. I guess we'll never get her apology now, though will we?"

"How is Edward? Was he very upset?" What I was really asking was if he was upset enough to kill Penney Sellers. But I couldn't ask the question. Mostly because I didn't believe it for a minute.

"He was angry. As angry as I've ever seen him." She shook her head. "She attacked his pride. Insulted his abilities as a provider. She couldn't have wounded him more if she'd stabbed him in the heart."

"When did this happen?" I asked her, praying she'd tell me it had been last week.

"Yesterday. Around nine o'clock in the morning." She shook her head. "Edward was so upset he climbed into the car and drove off. I didn't see him until seven o'clock last night. But thank heavens he'd calmed down by then."

"He left the house?" I asked, trying to keep my voice calm. Not an easy task since her words had made me see stars. Edward Johnston was unaccounted for during the time Penney Sellers was killed. According to his wife, he was definitely angry enough to do something he'd later regret. "Do you know where he went?"

"I don't. He's always done that, though. When he's upset he just gets into his car and drives. It soothes him. When we lost our sweet Peanuts, he drove all the way to Nashville before turning around and coming home." She shook her head at the memory, a sad smile playing across her lips.

"Did he call you or anything while he was driving?" I was asking out of desperation. I needed something to use to cross him off the suspect list.

"I'm afraid not." Her wistful gaze slid to me and sharpened. "And you'll want to know where I was when that horrible woman was killed too, won't you, dear?"

I blinked in surprise. She hadn't been fooled for a minute by my attempt to get information without accusing them. I'd thought I'd been clever enough to fool her. But Belle Johnston had taught elementary school music for several decades. Of course, she was too sharp to be played. "I'm sorry."

She fluttered her fingers. "Don't be. I completely understand. If someone had been murdered here, I'd want to get to the bottom of it too. Unfortunately, I can't help you. I was here, alone in the house, all day yesterday. I have no alibi. And I can assure you, when I heard how that terrible woman had insulted my sweet husband, I was angry enough to do her violence."

I swallowed hard, my stomach twisting with nerves. "Did you?"

She sighed. "No. I didn't kill her. But I won't tell you I'm sorry someone else did."

CHAPTER ELEVEN

Hal called me as I was heading home. "Hey," I answered.

"What's up? I saw you'd called a few times."

"I just wanted to invite you to go with me to the Johnstons'."

There was a beat of silence. "Please tell me you didn't go there alone."

"Hal, they're almost eighty. I think I can handle them."

He sighed. I pictured him rubbing his face in disgust. "Okay. Well, what did you find out?"

I gave him a quick rundown on my meeting with Mrs. Johnston. "I don't like that neither of them has an alibi."

"You think they might have killed her?"

I frowned, but only because, despite the ridiculousness of it, I couldn't entirely discount the possibility. "I don't know."

"Okay, well, we'll dig deeper on that in the morning." He hesitated. "Would you like to come over for a while? I've got a great bottle of wine I've been dying for you to try."

It was so tempting. But I wasn't ready to pretend things were normal for us. "I can't. I have the cat. She's probably feeling lonely and scared right about now."

"I'm pretty sure demons don't get lonely."

"Har. I'll see you in the morning?"

"I'll bring breakfast."

"Night, Hal."

"Night, Joey. I miss you."

I hung up before I could give in to the sad note in his voice. I knew I was being hard on him. And with a little time and distance, I was starting to see that I'd overreacted to finding out about the cabin.

But I was having trouble seeing the path out of it. And I hadn't been lying about the cat. I felt like I'd been neglecting her.

I pulled into my driveway, and Caphy jumped up from her spot in the center of the back seat. Her muscular tail smacked the seat a few times.

"We're home, Caphy girl."

She lunged between the front seats and swiped a wide, wet tongue over my cheek. I laughed, rubbing dog spit off my face with one arm.

I parked and she leaped out when I opened the door, hightailing it toward the pond, barking. I thought about calling her back, knowing she'd probably disturb the crime scene tape Arno'd left behind. Then I realized there was no way for him to control the scene. No doubt there'd been countless critters scampering along the grassy bank since he'd erected it.

He had what he needed from the scene anyway. He'd found the murder weapon, and they'd found no footprints in the hard earth of the bank. I'd overheard them talking about the lack of evidence when I'd been skulking on the porch like a piece of furniture, hoping they wouldn't notice me and make me leave.

I opened the front door, leaving it slightly ajar for Caphy's return. I'd check on the cat and sit with her for a while if she'd let me, then make Caphy and me some dinner. I'd take a long bath and make it an early night. I had a mystery from one of my favorite authors waiting for me in my room.

With that happy plan in place, I dropped my keys on a table in the foyer and trotted up the stairs to LaLee's temporary digs. I listened at the door for a moment and didn't hear anything. Then I realized that thinking I'd hear her was stupid. Unlike big, clumsy pit bulls who lumbered and danced through life, bouncing off everything they passed, cats never made any noise unless they were communicating.

I opened the door a crack, peeked through to the bed and kennel, and saw nothing. I pushed it wider, "LaLee..."

A slim, black and taupe blur shot past my feet and down the stairs, rocketing through the front door and outside before I could so much as yelp.

With a muttered expletive, I flew down the steps after her, calling her name even while I knew the feline would totally ignore me. She clearly hated me.

I shot outside, my feet pounding on the porch just as the blur tore around the side of the house and disappeared in the evergreens clustered ten feet away. I called Caphy and took off running after her.

It wasn't until a minute later, when Caphy shot past me, head high and eyes bright with the thrill of the chase, that I realized my mistake. I probably shouldn't have invited my dog to join the chase. The cat was more likely to run away from the exuberant pitty than she was from me. And if Caphy got too excited chasing LaLee, she might hurt the cat.

"Caphy, come!" At first, she ignored me. But when my command turned shrill, to her credit, she took pity on me and stopped, watching me run her way with her tongue lolling out the side of her mouth. "Good girl," I told her as I loped up and scratched her between her droopy ears. "Heel."

She fell in alongside me and, though I could tell it was

killing her to regulate her speed to mine, stayed pretty much to heel as I'd commanded until we reached the big, overgrown field in the back twenty acres of my property.

My gaze automatically skimmed away from the long, narrow field where my parents had met their violent ends. I'd let the grass runway return to its wild state, allowing the stalks of milkweed and wide green blades of grass to cover the torn earth and pieces of refuse that were left behind when my dad's beloved Cessna had hit a large rock that shouldn't have been there and went tail over nose, crashing into pieces as it skidded slowly to a stop.

My traitorous brain recalled the horrible sight...a piece of wing...a chunk of fuselage...and the oily pools of fuel and oil that had leaked from the battered corpse of the small plane.

I shook my head to dispel the horror of that night, my nose twitching under the remembered stench of smoke and burning fuel.

Caphy was whining at the door to the big outbuilding where my dad had housed his plane. The hangar. She scratched at a small metal door, her tail drooping.

My Uncle Devon had hidden out in that building for a while, unable to put my parents' deaths fully behind him and with some twisted sense of loyalty that included keeping a promise to my dad to watch out for me.

My eyes teared up as I remembered the last time I'd seen him, and my gaze slid to the distant tree line, where he'd stood not too far from the coyotes he'd befriended over the years.

I blinked, panic rising.

Coyotes! I had to find LaLee.

But even as I had the thought, I knew the chances of that were almost nil. If the cat didn't want me to find her, I wouldn't find her.

Angry tears slid from my eyes. I dropped down onto a

stump and let them flow. How did I get myself into these things?

Caphy's shrill voice filtered through my pity party and I looked over as she warbled hysterically, her paws digging frantically in the dirt in front of the door. She was going to rip a claw on the concrete if she didn't stop.

"Caphy! Stop that."

A coyote yipped in the distance, followed almost immediately by a series of answering yips. Gooseflesh rose on my arms. It was the sound of a pack announcing prey. I took off running toward the sound, picking my way carefully through the overgrown field.

When I hit the other side, I ran along the tree line, calling the cat's name in a shrill, desperate tone.

The yipping stopped and, as I pushed through the trees, I saw several of the beasts loping away from me, across the next field. My heart thudded as I spotted something furry hanging from one of their mouths.

"Oh no!" I wailed out. "LaLee!"

I dropped to my knees, despair tugging the starch from my legs. I sobbed loudly, feeling totally out of control. The cat had hated me. She'd been kind of a pain in the patooty. But she'd counted on me to keep her safe, and I'd failed.

A new wave of sobbing shook me, bowing my back. I thought I might just shrivel up on the ground and totally lose my mind.

What a horrible way to die...

"Yeow!"

I was so deep into my devastation it took my mind a second to wrap itself around what I'd heard.

"Yeow..." Something soft and warm touched my arm. I jumped, startling the blue-eyed cat sitting daintily beside me, her long tail tucked around her brown body.

"LaLee!"

She blinked at the shrieking quality of my voice, moving quickly to her feet and walking a few feet away. Her tail snapped with irritation. Her eyes narrowed on me as if she thought I'd lost my mind. "I can't believe you're alive," I told her, fighting to regain control of my emotions.

The grass beyond the trees thrashed violently, and I started. *Caphy*!

LaLee's head snapped around and she tensed, her body rigid and a low growl rumbling from her narrow brown chest.

I shoved slowly to my feet, cognizant of the need not to spook the cat. "Caphy, girl," I said softly walking toward the thrashing sound in the hopes of grabbing my dog before she saw LaLee.

As I emerged from the trees, I spotted Caphy's wide, blonde form bounding across the field. She was a mere ten feet away and closing fast. I stepped toward her, holding out my hands. "Caphy, come!"

She sprang toward me, mouth wide in a toothy grin. I kept moving in her direction, arms outstretched. "Come on, girl.

She got within five feet of me and screeched to a halt, her body going stiff.

I tried to reach for her, but she evaded my grip and took off like a shot toward the spot where I'd left LaLee.

"No!" Swinging around, I dug in my heels and ran after her, my heart pounding. "Caphy, no!"

She disappeared into the trees. A beat later there was a snarl, a hiss and a yowl. And, finally, a pain filled cry.

I ran faster, horrible thoughts flitting through my mind. Caphy was a sweet girl, but when something ran from her she chased it, and I wasn't sure she had the strength to keep her prey drive in check in the heat of excitement.

I burst through the last line of trees, fully expecting to see a dead cat lying at Caphy's feet. What I actually saw made my eyes go wide.

LaLee sat much as she had when gracing me with her presence. Her slender legs were straight and close against her body. Her tail wrapped tightly around them. Only the tip of the tail twitched with emotion. Her blue eyes, bright in the dark brown of her tiny face, were filled with hostility, but she didn't seem overly concerned about the cowering hulk of my sweet pibl a few feet away.

For her part, Caphy was hunkered down, her big body trembling and her ears pinched back as she observed the feline interloper with an uncertain gaze. The tip of her light brown nose glistened with a shiny drop of blood.

"Oh, Caphy girl." She shivered and her tail gave a half-hearted wag, but she kept her attention on the cat, as if she could keep her locked into place with the force of her gaze.

LaLee was one smart cat. She hadn't run from Caphy. That had probably saved her life. But more importantly, she'd drawn first blood. If things worked as they generally did in the natural world, her dominance had been settled.

I didn't like that my dog had been usurped in her own territory. But if it kept them both safe until I could find LaLee a home, I could live with it. I sighed my relief. "Come on, girls. How about we go home now?"

CHAPTER TWELVE

Getting home was slow going, with Caphy and I stepping lightly to avoid startling the cat. Of course, we had different reasons for wanting to keep from startling LaLee. Mine was because I was trying to earn her trust so she'd follow me home.

Judging by the way my dog was trying to insert herself into my thigh, I was guessing she didn't want to experience the business end of the cat's claws again.

I reached down and scratched Caphy between the ears, keeping my hand on her head to let her know I'd protect her from the big, bad, ten-pound feline.

I was amazed the cat was following at all, but I could only assume she realized what a close call she'd had when she'd come upon the pack of coyotes.

Obviously, she wasn't stupid. Only arrogant, opinionated, and stubborn.

When we got back to the house, I was dismayed to realize I'd left the front door wide open. Not too smart given the fact that someone had already trespassed once to kill Penney Sellers and had possibly even come inside the house.

I sent Caphy into the house ahead of me, knowing she'd send out a vocal warning if something was awry inside. Then I turned to see if LaLee had followed us onto the porch. She sat in a dying ray of sun at the very end of the long porch, her gaze locked on mine and filled with suspicion.

"Are you going to come inside?" I asked softly. "It's not safe out here for you."

The cat broke eye contact and lifted a dainty paw, licking it as if she didn't have a care in the world.

Inside the house, Caphy's nails clicked across the foyer tiles. She stood looking at me, her tail wagging. Apparently, all was well. "Thanks, sweet girl."

The wagging tail increased its tempo.

I looked at the still-bathing cat. "We're going inside. I hope you'll join us." I felt only slightly silly talking to the cat as if she could understand me. There was something about the feline's demeanor that made me feel like she could understand at least some of what I was saying. I wondered if her previous owner had talked to her a lot.

I had trouble seeing Penney Sellers as a loving pet owner. But she'd had to love somebody, I guessed. Or something, besides money.

I ducked through the door and bent to kiss Caphy's wide head. "Let's go clean that scratch, Caphy girl."

With a final glare at the door, she fell into step beside me. Five minutes later, I saw the long, low shape of the Siamese cat easing past the kitchen door. I finished filling Caphy's water bowl and hurried to close the front door before LaLee could go back outside.

When I turned back around, I twitched in surprise.

LaLee was sitting right behind me, staring at me through her expressive blue eyes. I got the sense she was letting me know she could have escaped if she'd chosen to.

"Okay, message received. You're an alien from another

planet, and you're smarter than anybody," I told her, frowning. "Now, do you think you could bend that stick in your butt enough to follow me into the kitchen and eat?"

She opened her mouth and gave a throaty yowl. I decided to take it as agreement. I knew when she came into the kitchen because Caphy stopped licking her bowl and scooted under the table, laying her head on her paws and watching the cat as if she were a ninja warrior sent to eradicate all pibls from existence.

"You two need to get along. Just for a little while."

LaLee yowled again, her tail held high and twitching with irritation.

"You're wrong about Caphy, Miss LaLee. She's a very sweet girl."

The cat's response was nearly a growl it was so low and grumbly.

I pulled a can of soft cat food out of the cabinet and opened it, scooping some into a bowl and placing it in front of LaLee. She looked at it and then smacked the edge of the bowl with her paw, making it rock and nearly tip over.

My cell phone rang. I grabbed it off the counter. It was Arno. "Hey."

"Hey, Joey. I was just calling to find out what you ended up doing with that cat."

"Why? Feeling guilty?"

"Joey." His voice was filled with disgust, but the beats of silence that followed told me I'd hit the nail on the head. "I do feel bad that I can't do more."

"Can't or won't?" I asked. I knew it was kind of mean, but I couldn't help twisting the knife a bit. He'd been such a jerk about helping me.

"Can't. I wasn't lying, Joey. I'm not set up to take in stray animals."

LaLee gave the bowl of food a tentative sniff and then

tapped a bit of it out onto the floor with her paw. She sniffed it again and then, with obvious reluctance, tasted it.

It didn't come back out again, so I guessed she didn't hate it. "Whatever. She's here with me. Caphy's already got a hole in her nose."

He sighed. "I guess I could take her myself."

LaLee lifted her head, narrowing her expressive blue eyes at me as if she understood what we were discussing. A wave of sadness made my chest tight. "It's nice of you to offer..."

"Well, I don't want Caphy to get beat up." His voice held a note of humor, and my lips twitched.

LaLee's eyes narrowed another fraction. I frowned, wondering why I wasn't jumping at the chance to unload her. For some reason, the idea didn't appeal. I realized how hard it would be on her to be moved again. And it was highly doubtful Arno would understand her unique temperament. I pictured them in a standoff, eyeing each other with hostility across the room.

I sighed, shaking my head. "No. Thanks for offering. But I'll keep her for now. I think we're starting to come to an understanding." I glanced at Caphy—still hunkered under the table, watching the cat—and silently wished for her forgiveness.

"You sure?"

LaLee started to eat again. It occurred to me she might be an alien after all. "Yep. How's the investigation going?"

"Not great. Our suspect pool is large."

"Yeah. I got that feeling from the few people I spoke to. Ms. Sellers was not a popular woman."

"No. And I don't get what she was doing, trying to list everything in town. She couldn't possibly have buyers for all the homes and businesses she wanted to list."

"Hal and I had the exact same thought. I guess she wouldn't necessarily have to have buyers. The article in the paper and the new subdivision are bringing a lot of potential buyers into *Deer Hollow*. It would have been a calculated risk."

"Yeah. I guess. I don't get the sense from her partner that she knew what Sellers was up to though. Don't you find that strange?"

"It is strange." I frowned, thinking of the slamming door when I went to visit the realtor. "Is there a third realtor in that practice?" I asked.

"Not that I know of. Why?"

"No reason. I just thought maybe another opinion on that would be helpful."

I thought of Hal's speculation after visiting Scott Abels. "Did Hal tell you about the title theft angle?"

"He did. I'm looking into it now. I have to tell you. I'm shocked by how easy it is to steal someone's home title."

"That's not very comforting."

"No. It's not. When things slow down, I'm going to look into title insurance myself."

"Do you think that's what Penney Sellers was into? She certainly seemed to live above a realtor's salary."

"Could be. But not necessarily. She was a very successful realtor."

"Seriously?"

"Yep. I did some background on her. She was the leading real estate salesperson in the state of Indiana for the last five years. She sold a lot of properties. My understanding is a large part of her success came from cold-calling homeowners like she'd been doing here."

"I can't believe that worked for her."

"Well, I'm guessing it worked better in the city than it would down here in Bumpkin town."

I chuckled.

"Is your boyfriend there? I need to speak to him about something."

"Hal's not here. I just spoke with him though, so you can probably catch him if you call." I hesitated a minute, knowing he was going to shoot down the request I was about to make, but unable to stop myself from making it. "What do you need? If you want him to question someone, I'd be happy to help."

"Nice try, Joey. I'll see you around. Stay out of trouble. And I mean that literally."

I stuck my tongue out at the phone after he disconnected. It was childish, I knew, but it made me feel better. Shivering, I realized the kitchen had grown cold since the sun went down. I tugged a sweater off one of the hooks near the door and wished I could remember where I'd left that second leash.

I came up with nothing. Rehanging the sweater, I decided to opt for a long, hot bath instead and headed upstairs to my room.

Maybe if I stopped trying so hard, the memory would come back to me.

~

True to his word, Hal showed up the next morning with bagels and cream cheese and fresh fruit in the form of mixed berries and melon.

I greeted him at the door with a smile and snatched the bag of bagels, opening it to inhale the sweet, doughy fragrance. "Mm, I'm starving."

He grabbed the bag and tugged, and since I wasn't letting go unless my life depended on it, I came with it, bumping up against his broad chest and giving a surprised little gasp of pleasure.

"Morning," he said in a husky voice. His lips found mine

and lingered there, curling my bare toes and making my stomach jump with pleasure.

When he broke the kiss, I stood with my eyes closed for a few beats, just letting the deliciousness of his greeting flow over me.

The mood was broken by the sound of paws thundering across the upstairs floor. My eyes popped open as Caphy, a devil-eyed feline hot on her tail, bounded down the steps, tail tucked and ears pinned back.

She leaped off the bottom step and threw on the brakes, skidding across the foyer floor and into Hal's jeans-clad legs. If he'd been a smaller man he'd have gone down under the assault. As it was, he wobbled slightly and then reached down to wrap his arms around my dog, hefting her off the ground as the cat slid to a graceful stop mere inches from his feet.

LaLee gave a throaty yowl and snapped her tail a few times before changing direction, rubbing against my calf as she headed toward the kitchen.

I looked at Hal and my quivering pibl. I grinned. "You're pathetic, Cacophony."

She whined softly, licking her lips and then swiping a wide, pink tongue over Hal's cheek.

He scowled. "I'm drenched."

Giggling, I motioned toward the kitchen, hugging my bag o' bagels. "Come on. She'll feel better after she has a bagel with cream cheese."

Hal settled Caphy back onto her feet and followed me.

Not an easy task, given that he had seventy pounds of pitty glued to his legs.

CHAPTER THIRTEEN

"Where are we off to today?" I asked Hal as I speared the last piece of watermelon from my bowl.

He wiped his fingers with a napkin and sat back. "I'm thinking we should talk to George Shulz."

"The lawyer who handled the sale of Uncle Dev's cabin to you?"

He nodded.

"Why?"

Hal sipped from his steaming mug of black coffee. "Because he might know where Devon is. Max's words stuck with me. She's right. If Devon thought Penney Sellers was a threat to you, he'd do just about anything to stop her."

"Including murder?" I asked, incredulous. "I don't believe that."

"I'm not sure you really know him."

Irritation flared, but I held my tongue for a minute, forcing myself to consider his charge. As the initial anger passed, I realized he was right. I'd never known the real Devon Little. He'd been a figment of my childhood impressions and then, after my parents died, a gossamer thread that tied me to their memory. "Okay. I'll give you that. Still…"

He settled his mug on the table. "I'm not saying I believe he did it, Joey. I'm just saying it's worth exploring. If nothing else, we can rule him out as a suspect."

I didn't like it, but I couldn't fault his reasoning. "Okay. Let's go see George Shulz. I have to admit, after seeing Max grimace when you said his name, I'm kind of interested in meeting him."

"Yeah, well, don't get too excited. You're going to want to pinch his head off after five minutes."

The lawyer's office was located on one of the short, dead-end streets that jutted from *Main Street* in *Deer Hollow*. It was a tiny, yellow clapboard house with a winding brick sidewalk leading to a dark green door.

The yard was well-trimmed. The house was freshly painted, and the sidewalk looked new. Still, the house gave off a slightly shabby air. Like, if it had shoulders they'd be rounded and drooping. And if it had hair, it would be lank and stringy.

A large, gold and black sign in the yard proclaimed it the *Shulz Law Practice*, with George Shulz's name and letters spelled out in six-inch-high letters.

Like the house, the sign looked as if it might have barely survived a zombie apocalypse, its body tilting ever so slightly windward, scarred and chipped.

I couldn't help wondering if the owner of the practice would be equally weary looking.

Hal slid me a look as he opened the front door. "Gird your loins," he murmured softly.

I grinned, wondering what it was about George Shulz that

made him such a difficult character to be around. I had my suspicions. But I was about to learn how wrong I could be.

George Shulz wasn't your typical arrogant, condescending lawyer type. He was more a mix of the grumpy neighbor and Hannibal Lecter.

The interior of the office looked like the site of a level five hurricane. Papers mounded every surface, interspersed like fillings on an ugly sandwich between binders dressed in a thousand hastily scribbled stickies.

The walls were covered in a mismatched array of book-shelves, some wood and some metal. Some of the shelving looked new. Some looked like it might have made the trip to the continent on a Viking ship, with unidentifiable stains and a tattered appearance consistent with that impression.

The room smelled like cat urine, mildew and other even less pleasant things. The reason for the first of those smells was easily uncovered as a fat, black and white feline wandered past, turning to glare at us and voice its displeasure that we'd intruded on its sanctuary. From high atop the worst looking example of book-shelvery, a thin, gray cat groomed its paws and ignored us completely. A strident hiss drew my attention to the coffee maker on a battered old cabinet across the room, where an orange striped feline observed us with a level of hostility I was pretty sure we hadn't earned.

In the small, equally cluttered conference room through the door to our immediate right, two more cats lounged on a claw-scarred wooden table, and another was draped over one of the stained kitchen chairs shoved beneath it.

Hal sniffed and then sneezed violently several times, until I was worried for his safety. I touched his arm. "Maybe you should wait outside."

He shook his head, pulling a hankie from his pocket and loudly blowing his nose. "I'll be okay as soon as the antihistamines kick in."

I looked around with a frown. "Where's Mr. Shulz?"

A flushing noise offered a disgusting response to my question, and a door beside one of the metal shelves opened with a bang.

I flinched, my OCD kicking in. There definitely hadn't been enough time between the flush and the opening of the door for the man blinking at us from the doorway to have washed up. I shoved my hands into the pockets of my jeans in self-defense.

No way was I shaking his hand.

As it turned out, there were no worries on that score. George Shulz seemed disinclined to come any closer. Instead, he stood there glaring at us like one of his cats. "What?" he finally asked.

Hal's beautiful lips twitched with humor. "Mr. Shulz, do you remember me?"

I thought that was a strange question but realized Hal had cause to wonder when the man turned a blank expression to him. "Thomas Beauregard. Murder one. Guilty as charged but a darn good liar." He shook his head, the greasy mop of hair glued around his face not even moving at the action. "Worst client I ever had. You deserved that prison sentence."

I gasped, turning to Hal with a shocked gaze.

He lifted one midnight eyebrow. "Nope. Try again."

Shulz cocked a bony hip and narrowed his gaze on Hal. "Peter Grenache. Forty counts of robbery. Unhygienic in the extreme. Most unpleasant fellow. I didn't appreciate being threatened with that knife. Scoundrel."

If George Shulz thought Peter Grenache was unhygienic, I hoped I never came within ten miles of the guy.

Hal sighed. "Not even close. Give it another go."

Impatience made me twitch. I opened my mouth to try to shorten the process, but Hal lifted a hand to stop me. "Trust me," he murmured. "This is the way it has to be."

I snapped my lips closed and gave a weary sigh.

Shulz took two steps closer and looked down his stubby, round nose at Hal, his shaggy brows lifting as he gave him a thorough once over. "Ah. Hal Amity. Arrogant and impatient. Purchased a home he had no right owning. Usurper."

I gave Hal a look. He chuckled. "Got it in three. You're improving."

Shulz's thin lips twisted with disgust. "Your condescension is not appreciated." He looked at me. "Why are you here?"

Good manners had my hand twitching out of my pocket in an unconscious movement to offer a handshake before I remembered I'd rather be murdered with a thousand pickle forks. I decided to give him my stats in a language he'd understand. "Joey Fulle. Unrepentant busybody. Never met you before and probably never will again. Looks great in tee-shirts and fringed jean shorts."

Shulz stared at me a long moment, his mouth working as if he were trying to chew up my words. Finally, he frowned. "Incorrect. Joey Fulle. Daughter of Brent and Joline Fulle, deceased. Unindicted smugglers. Horrible people. Deserved their fate."

Hal was right. I did want to pinch off his head. Except that would mean I'd have to touch him. My hands flew out of my pockets and transformed into fists. I'd never punched anybody in my life, but I was about to do it. The horrible man standing across the room deserved to have his face dented, and I was just the woman to do it.

Fortunately for Shulz—and probably everybody involved —Hal reached over and wrapped a big, warm hand around one of my fists and gave it a squeeze. I took a deep breath, striving for calm, and then settled for a verbal punch, which was less likely to get me thrown into the *Deer Hollow* jail. "You're a jerk. My parents were wonderful people. No wonder all your clients threaten to kill you."

Shulz shrugged, his blank expression unchanged. "Not all of them. Approximately sixty-three percent threaten violence. Five percent cower in my presence. One percent call the police and fifteen percent try to get me committed."

I did a quick mental calculation. "What about the other sixteen percent?"

He shrugged. "They leave as soon as they see the office."

"Understandable," I replied, giving the room another quick look.

"I'm afraid you're wasting your time insulting me, Miss Joey Fulle. I'm a sociopath. I don't care what you or anyone else thinks."

"I need to ask you about Devon Little," Hal said as I chewed on the lawyer's astounding admission. How was it possible for a sociopath to work as a lawyer? Then I realized that made as much sense as him being a serial killer, the usual profession of sociopaths.

Shulz stared at Hal for a moment. "There's no reason for me to tell you anything about Devon Little. He no longer owns your house."

"Ah, but there is a reason. I have questions about...ah...the heating system. I need to find out what the warranty is."

Shulz lifted his hands. "Not my problem. Don't care. Go away."

My hands found their way into fists again.

"What if I can make it your problem?" Hal said quickly, giving me a quelling look.

"I'm listening."

"Mr. Little is a person of interest in a murder. If I tell Deputy Willager you've been in contact with your client, he'll be all over you like a cheap suit.

Shulz thought about that for a moment. "Why would you do that?"

Hal shrugged. "Why wouldn't we?"

As a self-professed sociopath, I figured Shulz should understand that simple concept. Apparently, I figured right.

"I don't know his present location."

"Then give us the last location you know. It's important that we find him," I said.

Shulz stared at me a long moment, gaze speculative, and then nodded. He moved to the paper-laden desk in the center of the overcrowded room and jotted something onto a sticky, shoving it toward Hal. "Now leave."

"Happily," I told him. But I didn't quite make it out of the room unscathed. Shulz's cold, unfeeling voice stopped me as Hal pulled the door open. "She could be with you now," he said.

I frowned. "Who?"

"Your mother. She chooses not to be. She never wanted you."

Though I knew he was lying—my mother was dead and couldn't choose to be with me at all—his words stabbed into me like a blade, slicing my heart in half. They cut way too close to home...to my deepest fears.

There was actual, physical pain from his hateful statement. I found it hard to breathe. "Shut up," I wheezed out, wishing my voice didn't sound so strangled.

Hal touched my arm, turning to give Shulz one last glare, which, if it had been directed at me, would have made my blood run cold. "Let's go, Joey. He's just being an ass."

He didn't have to ask me twice.

I huddled in my seat, too unhappy to talk as Hal drove us out of *Deer Hollow*. He let me brood for a while and then reached over and squeezed my hand. "He was lying, Joey."

I shrugged, trying to pretend I didn't care and that Shulz's words hadn't cut me to the bone. But I doubted my pretense was very convincing since I was pretty sure I had massive internal bleeding from his taunt.

"He likes to hurt people. He thrives on it."

I frowned. "There's one thing I don't get."

"What's that?" he asked me, still holding my hand.

"He has cats."

After a beat, Hal glanced my way, confusion on his handsome face. "He does."

"What I mean is, aren't sociopaths generally cruel to animals? Don't they torture them and stuff? Why would he have them at all, and so many of them at that?"

"One, I don't think he's a true sociopath. Not in the clinical sense of the word. He's just a really mean person and he uses that as an excuse to get away with his cruelty. And, secondly, I'm pretty sure he has all those cats just to annoy people. I don't care how much you like cats. When you squash that many of them into a small space, the result isn't pleasant."

My nose wrinkled in scent memory. "You aren't kidding. It smelled like a meth lab in there."

He grinned. Giving my hand a squeeze, he finally released it. I felt the loss of his heat and his touch like a physical thing. "Are you up for a visit to this location?"

I glanced at the sticky he held out, taking it from him to look at the address. "This is off *Highway 37*. There's nothing but trees and farmland out there."

"I'm not expecting much," Hal told me. "Devon's probably long gone by now. But we need to follow it up."

I agreed. We needed to follow up. Just in case my dad's best friend was feeling cocky and didn't bother relocating after dealing with his sleazy lawyer. But, like Hal, I didn't have very high hopes for the outcome.

Boy was I wrong.

CHAPTER FOURTEEN

The ramshackle barn huddling in the distance appeared to be the only structure on the property. Hal pulled the Escalade off *Highway 37* and stopped it when the short gravel drive ended. We sat, staring at the barn, seeing the half-collapsed roof and hole-riddled walls of weathered gray wood.

There was no fencing around the calf-tall grass, and I didn't see any livestock. Nothing moved in the shadowed doorway, which was half-open and sagging like the rest of the structure. "I doubt anybody's living in that," I told Hal.

He frowned. "That's probably a good bet." He glanced at me. "You want to wait here while I give it a quick look?"

Reaching for the door handle, I shook my head. "Not a chance."

He smiled. "I should have known." But he glanced at my low-cut pull-on sneaks. "You're going to get your shoes dirty."

"They'll wash." I climbed out, slamming the car door before he could talk me out of coming. I couldn't explain why, but I felt an almost overwhelming urge to check out the dilapidated barn. It could have been just my fascination with old barns. I'd always loved them, to the point where I'd been mad at my dad for two weeks when he'd torn down the one on our property that had once stood where his hangar now was.

But it was more than that.

As I stared at the building, my heart started to beat really fast. The sun rose up just behind the ancient structure, painting its old walls in gold and creating a halo-like effect. I found myself walking in that direction without conscious knowledge of having moved.

I was dimly aware of Hal calling my name.

A moment later he came up beside me, wrapping a hand around my elbow. "You know there are probably snakes in this grass."

I twitched, my feet jolting to a stop. "Ugh!"

He grinned. "Just watch where you step."

I picked my way carefully through the rest of the tall grass and Hal pulled the sagging barn door open. It groaned and caught in several places before he managed to wrench it open enough for us to pass easily through. We stopped just inside the door, our eyes adjusting to the dimmer light inside. The sun filtering through the broken walls and roof painted golden lines across the dirt floor, gilding random strands of straw and highlighting things better left unnoticed.

I frowned at the dried-up husk of a dead rat and fought the urge to step back through the door.

Hal moved into the barn, his tall frame dwarfed by the high, peaked roofline. On one end, a fractured wooden ladder climbed to a loft with moldy hay spilling over its edge like ugly lace. On the wall beneath the loft, a plain wooden door stood slightly ajar. I headed for that.

As I grew closer, I found that my chest had tightened. I wondered if I was having an asthma attack. I'd had asthma as a kid but had largely outgrown it. I rarely suffered from its effects anymore, and when I did, it was just a small sense of pressure that quickly dissipated.

But the feeling making it hard to breathe wasn't going away. I stopped in front of the door, my hand outstretched to grab the ancient brass knob, and thought I could hear the quickening of someone's breath on the other side of the door.

I considered calling Hal over, just in case, but decided against it. I was letting my imagination run away with me. There was nothing behind that door but dust and dead spiders. Squaring my shoulders, I reached out and pulled it open.

My heartbeat stuttered. I gasped, one hand reaching out to grab the door frame.

My knees buckled.

If it hadn't been for the sudden arrival of Hal behind me, his strong arms encircling my waist, I might have hit the ground.

My head started to shake and my lips parted, the denial I wanted to scream dying before the words could emerge.

Shock turned the edges of my world gray as I stared at the woman standing in the middle of the tiny, disheveled tack room.

She stood tall and lean, hair swept back from her still pretty face in a ponytail that made her look ten years younger than her fifty years. She looked slightly ruffled around the edges. As if she'd spent too much time in filthy, decaying barns. But the gentle smile I remembered all too well transformed the roughness into a regal kind of beauty.

"Hello, sweetie."

I swallowed, my lips slamming closed as shock made stars burst before my eyes. I shook my head. "It can't be."

"I'm sorry, honey," Joline Fulle said softly. "I can explain everything."

I sincerely doubted that. But, since I'd thought she was

dead for over two years, I was definitely interested in where she'd been. Why she hadn't told me, her only child, that she was alive. And why she hadn't cared enough to consider the pain I was suffering because of her loss.

She could be with you now... She chooses not to be. She never wanted you.

I shook my head to dispel Schulz's cruel taunts from my mind as she began.

"I was only trying to keep you safe."

I must have whimpered because Hal's arms tightened around me. "I think we should do this somewhere else."

I glanced up, my gaze catching on his and seeing the pity there. I bristled. I didn't need his pity. It made me feel pathetic. A dupe. A pawn. "No. There's nothing she could say that I'd be interested in hearing." I pulled away from Hal and shoved past him to the door. I stopped to look back to my mother. "Do you have any idea what you put me through? I almost died from grief. You could have saved me that. But you obviously decided I wasn't important enough..."

She took a step closer, her hand outstretched and a pleading look on her face. "That's not true, sweetie. Hear me out, please."

I jerked my head in the negative. "I don't know why you're skulking around here. There's nothing left for you in *Deer Hollow*. You should leave."

I nearly ran from the barn, tears flowing so fast and furiously they nearly blinded me. A bird rose into the air with a surprised squawk as I plunged from the dim light of the decaying structure into the sunlight. A soft breeze pushed at my hair as I ran. A sob tore from my throat. I didn't get far. Halfway to the car, I dropped to my knees in the grass, panting and sobbing.

Moments later, I'd forced myself to calm down.

The soft swish of footsteps behind me gave warning that I

wasn't alone. I didn't look up, assuming it was Hal. "I want to go home."

There was a long moment of silence. Then a soft voice said. "I lost him that night, Joey. The man I'd always loved. I lost him more than once."

I stiffened, my head coming up. I didn't want to hear the story she needed to tell me. I wanted to run away from it. From her. From the rejection she represented.

But I couldn't move. My muscles locked and I sat there, unable to escape.

"I wanted to die too. I probably would have if it wasn't for you. For Devon."

I blinked in surprise, finally turning to look at her. "Don't lie to me."

She sank slowly into the grass, shaking her head. "It's true. Devon saved me that night. He dragged me away and hid me in that cabin for weeks."

I frowned. "Hid you? Why?"

"You're a smart girl, sweetie. Tell me you didn't have questions about the crash?"

"I did, but..."

She nodded. "Someone put that rock in the grass that night. Someone made sure your father's plane would hit it in the dark."

"Who?"

She shrugged. "I don't know the answer to that. We thought, at first that it had something to do with the job we were on..."

"The painting?" I asked. "Hal and I solved that mystery."

"Not the painting. That was a small problem. One which your father was trying to fix in the midst of a much bigger issue."

"I don't understand." I turned around, crossed my legs

and leaned my forearms on my knees, caught up in her story despite myself. "What bigger issue?"

"A friend of your father's from Indianapolis asked us to help. To use our network to move someone to safety."

"Some*one*?" I asked incredulously. "You moved a person?"

Joline Fulle's lips tightened. "A woman. The girlfriend of Garland Medford, a criminal who has ties to drugs, sex trafficking, and murder. Medford's organization is wide and well-connected. Your dad's friend believed Garland even had an informant in the US Marshals Service."

"Witness Protection...?"

"Not safe," my mother responded

I frowned. "So, you delivered this woman that night and then what? The bad guy found out and made the plane crash?"

She looked down at her hands. "I don't know the details."

I bit back frustration. "You know you're alive. And you know my father isn't. And you know..." My heart skipped a beat. "Is Arno in on this?"

"Why would you ask that?"

"Because he reported two bodies in that crash. A man and a woman. He reported that *you* were in that crash."

My mother shrugged. "The woman was my size and had my coloring." She frowned, her cheeks pinkening. "I suppose he saw what he expected to see. There would have been no reason for him to look further."

I felt a stab of pity for her as she spoke. It couldn't be easy for her to discuss my father's death and realize that, for whatever reason, she'd escaped his fate.

Why had she? I asked myself. *Why hadn't she been in that plane with him?*

My mother's mouth tightened into a straight line. "Obviously, it wasn't me."

"Where were you that night?"

"I was there. Waiting for him to return. I was catching up on some paperwork in the office."

"So, you saw..."

A tear slid down her cheek. "If Devon hadn't been there, I'd probably have been blown up when the engine exploded. I was trying to get to your father..." She swallowed hard, her cheeks wet with silvery tears. "He stopped me. He dragged me away, screaming and fighting him with every step. He took me to his cabin and made me promise to stay there while he went to find out what was going on."

"You knew father was with someone in the plane that night."

"Yes."

"And you know who it was, don't you?"

She wouldn't meet my gaze. It was Hal who put the puzzle pieces together. "The dead woman was Garland Medford's girlfriend, wasn't it? The one you were supposed to hide?"

She didn't confirm his assumption, but the pain that flitted across her pretty face was confirmation enough. Instead of responding, she glanced his way. "Who are you?"

Hal tugged a business card out of the pocket of his jeans and handed it to her. "I'm a good friend of your daughter's. She and I have been looking into the murder of a local Realtor."

My mother stared at the card for a long moment, as if she struggled to understand the words and numbers typed across its front. Finally, she sighed. "I'm glad she has you."

Hal and I shared a look. She hadn't answered his question and that was all the answer we needed.

"Why?" I asked her. "Why was she in the plane and you weren't?"

A tear slid silently down my mother's cheek. "Because he was in love with her. And in the end, he decided being with her was more important than anything else."

CHAPTER FIFTEEN

I didn't believe for a moment that my mother's words were true. So, I ignored them, asking a more important question instead. "Why were they coming back?"

Her gaze slid to mine. She sniffled and scraped the back of her hand under her eyes. "I don't understand the question."

"Father and the woman. Why was he bringing her back here? I understood you were going to hide her."

Understanding lit her gaze. "Yes. The flight out was a ruse, meant to confuse Medford's people."

"You suspected they were watching the house?" Hal asked with a frown.

"Yes." She slid me a guilty look. "We were worried for your safety and wanted to draw them off. Your father filed a false flight pattern leading them to Wisconsin and then doubled back." She frowned. "I was supposed to be on the plane too but, at the last minute, he asked me to stay. That's when I knew he was in love with her. We'd never separated on a job before. We'd always been a team."

"Maybe he'd known it was dangerous," I told her gently. "Maybe he was trying to keep you safe."

Mother shook her head. "No. I knew then that they were going to run off somewhere together."

She sounded like a crazy woman. "But he came back. Doesn't that prove anything to you?" I asked.

"He came back because Devon radioed him and told him the ruse was blown. Your father's friend from Indy learned Garland knew what we were up to. He'd sent people to the location where your father had planned on landing to refuel. At that point, we didn't know how much of our plan Medford knew, so we had to scrap the whole thing. Your father and Devon decided the safest play was for them to return here and engage Plan B."

"That's why the landing on a stormy night," I said as one of the puzzle pieces fell into place.

She nodded. "He knew it was dangerous, but it also made our plan work better. They'd never assume he'd double back into the eye of the storm."

"Do you know how Medford found out?" Hal asked, his gaze narrowing with speculation.

"Devon and I have given it a lot of thought since that night. We believe Medford has someone here in *Deer Hollow*. Someone we'd never suspect who keeps his eyes and ears open and reports back to him."

"But you don't know who it is?"

She glanced at Hal. "I wish we did. Devon's been snooping around the edges, trying to figure it out, but so far whoever it is has been successful in keeping a low profile."

"So, what was Plan B?" I asked.

She shrugged. "We'd planned to move the woman to a safe spot here in *Deer Hollow*."

"But why here?" Hal asked. "That seems risky. Especially given the fact you believed Medford had a spy here."

"Yes, that made it riskier for sure. But we intended to

keep the operation really close. Only four people would know. My husband and I, Devon and the woman. And it was just temporary. We're good at moving goods, Mr. Amity. Brent and I have moved a lot of merchandise through the auction house. We deliver all around the world. Our plan was to deliver the woman via normal routes. We had it set up so that even we wouldn't know where she ended up."

"You created your own witness protection," I said, slightly in awe.

She nodded. "She would make the final leg on her own. Our people were to deliver her to an airport in New Mexico and she'd drive to her destination from there. She was the only one who knew what that destination was."

"Who bankrolled the operation?" Hal asked.

My mother's expression turned sly. "Let's just say she had friends in high places."

"I guess," he said, making my mom smile sadly.

She turned a frown on me. "How did you find me?"

"George Shulz," Hal told her. "We were looking for Devon Little."

A wary look flitted across her gaze. "Dev's not here."

"Why are *you* here, Mom?" I asked her. "In this horrible barn?"

She glanced back to the hulking structure, a secret smile playing across her lips. Finally, she pushed to her feet, brushing at some loose grass on her calves. "Come on. I'll show you."

As we followed her back into the barn, she shook out the peasant skirt that floated around her slender legs. "We put this together in the weeks before Sasha came to us..."

"Sasha?" I asked.

Her lips compressed. "The woman we were hiding."

Ahh...

"This was where we were going to keep her until we thought it was safe to move her on."

I looked up at the hole-filled roof and down at the silty dirt floor, grimacing. "You didn't like her, huh?"

My mom chuckled, shoving open the tack room door. "It's not as bad as it looks." She moved toward the back wall and grabbed hold of a saddle rack hanging there. More saddle racks hung on either side of it, with tack-laden hooks four feet above on the same wall.

"She lifted the rack, and a soft whirring sound made me step back in surprise. To my amazement, a narrow space opened in the wall, as the ancient barn wood slid back behind the saddle racks and a brightly lit room opened up before our eyes.

Through the door was another room, one that was clean and bright and filled with the fresh scent of violets, my mother's favorite. She motioned toward the opening. "Welcome to my home."

I stepped through the opening into another world. The space was only about fifteen feet wide, but it looked as if it ran the length of the barn. The windows were high and covered in frilly cotton curtains that let in all the light. From outside, I guessed it would be impossible to see through them into the room.

The floor was covered in real wood flooring, wide planks in a golden oak color. The walls were brick, painted white and covered with an array of brightly-hued paintings. The paintings were of flowers and country scenes, rustic bridges arching over glistening creeks.

The furnishings were brass and wood, all antiques but restored, giving the space a cozy-chic look rather than a rustic one. A queen-sized bed dominated one end of the room, with brightly painted tables on either side that held tall metal and wood lamps with bright white shades. A round, wooden table and two iron chairs dominated the center, sitting atop a multi-colored round rag rug. Along the outside wall, a galley kitchen was bright and pleasant, with white cabinets, the doors inlaid with leaded glass, a charcoal gray stone countertop with black veining, and a white porcelain farmhouse sink. A small stainless-steel refrigerator and stove completed the space, with a matching microwave over the stove.

"What do you think?" my mom asked, smiling.

Despite my roiling thoughts and general feeling of confusion, I grinned. "It's beautiful."

"Electricity?" Hal asked, clearly looking past the aesthetics to the practical.

"Generator. Propane. Devon pays them in cash when they come to refill the tank. Completely untraceable."

"And from the outside..." I began.

"It looks like an old barn. We've even covered the glass in those windows with dirty, clouded plastic so they can't see the curtains."

"Amazing," I breathed. I shook my head. "This is genius."

"Thanks, honey. Your father and I worked on it together." A cloud fell over her face. "I miss him."

I reached out and grasped her hand. That simple touch ripped something open inside me that I'd twisted tightly shut to keep from losing my mind. Emotions swamped me, and I wobbled where I stood. It was as if I hadn't fully grasped that she was alive until that moment.

Tears slid down my cheeks.

My mom wrapped her arms around me and hugged me tight. I closed my eyes and let myself enjoy the moment.

There were still so many questions. And we still had the murder of Penney Sellers to figure out. But for just a moment,

I could enjoy being with my mom again...the woman whose loss had nearly taken me down completely.

If it hadn't been for Caphy...

I blinked, pulled away from my mom. "Caphy's gonna split something when she sees you."

She laughed, swiping at her own tears and sniffling. "I'm afraid that will have to wait. Though I'd give almost anything to see her too. I've missed her sweet, squishy little face."

She placed her hands on my cheeks, looking into my eyes. "But I've missed your beautiful face more. I love you, sweetie. I'm so sorry for the pain we caused you."

I nodded, too overcome with emotion to respond.

"Mrs. Fulle," Hal said.

We both looked at him in surprise. For a moment, I'd actually forgotten he was there.

"We need to know where Devon Little is."

I should have known Hal wouldn't be distracted from the job at hand. "Hal, maybe we should..."

My mom squeezed my hand. "No, sweetie, he's right. A woman has died. You need to find out who killed her." She looked at my PI. "But I can promise you it wasn't Dev. He wouldn't kill anybody."

"I would have believed that a few years ago, mom. But he's different now."

"Different, how?"

"Secretive, sneaky."

As soon as I said the words, I realized why. "He's been protecting you, hasn't he?"

"And you. He promised your father a long time ago that if anything ever happened to him, Dev would watch out for us. He's been true to that promise."

"That might be, Mrs. Fulle," Hal said. "But I still need to talk to him. I need you to tell me where he is."

She shook her head. "I don't know. Devon keeps his

whereabouts secret for just this reason. He moves around a lot. He's gotten very good at keeping a low profile."

Didn't I know it? The last time he'd shown up I'd found him by accident. He'd been living in the hangar...

I blinked. A memory surfaced that had me clamping my teeth down on my lip to keep from blurting out to Hal that I knew where my uncle was.

"If he's innocent he has nothing to fear in talking to us," Hal tried again.

But my mom stared back at him with a mulish look on her pretty face that I recognized all too well. "Devon wouldn't have killed that woman unless he was forced to do it to protect my daughter. And if he *has* done something to protect Joey, you're not going to talk me into turning on him."

Try as I might, I couldn't talk my mother into coming home with me. She insisted she was safe where she was and, more importantly, that I was safer with her there.

I finally left in a huff, the memory of just how stubborn she could be returning with a vengeance. "That woman!" I said to Hal as we climbed back into his car.

He wisely said nothing. When I looked at him, there was a tiny smile curving his lips. "What?"

He shook his head. "Uh-uh. I'm staying out of this."

"You're thinking the apple didn't fall far from the tree, aren't you?" I accused.

Hal made a zipping motion over his lips.

I expelled a frustrated breath.

"Well, we didn't find Devon," he finally said after a couple of minutes of silence.

His words reminded me of what I'd realized at my mother's place. I straightened in the seat. "Oh!"

He glanced over. "Oh?"

"I think I might know where he is."

"Really? Where?"

I smiled, feeling like the cat that had a helpless mouse in its sights. "Hiding in plain sight. Where else?"

CHAPTER SIXTEEN

I didn't have any better luck talking the cat into *not* accompanying us to the back forty than I had convincing my mother into anything.

The two of them must have shared a form in a previous life.

Hal, Caphy, LaLee, and I headed toward the defunct runway. Now that I knew the real situation with the crash, the area produced even more unsettling feelings in me when it came into sight.

"You think he's back in your dad's office?" Hal sounded disbelieving.

I didn't really blame him. Devon had been living like a homeless person in that small room when we'd found him before. It would seem unlikely he'd return to a previous haunt for fear he'd be caught by Deputy Arno. But Devon was both determined and unchanging. He clung to things he knew.

And there was one other little detail.

"Arno said Penney Sellers was killed with Caphy's leash." I glanced up at Hal as his eyes went wide. "But her leash is in my kitchen, hanging on the hook where I last put it."

"Then it was one that looked like hers? That would imply the killer was someone who knew you pretty well...well enough to match something kind of random...but it hardly points to Devon. In fact, since he hasn't really been in your life for a couple of years, it seems to me like it goes a long way toward proving it wasn't him."

I shook my head. "It's not that. When I found out the leash was used, I was trying to remember where I'd last seen my spare. I've always kept one in the house and one..."

"In your dad's office," Hal finished for me, nodding his head.

"Yep. The coyotes and Caphy's fascination with them are an issue back here. I'd sometimes leash her if it was getting dark, just in case. I didn't want her running off and getting herself into trouble."

"Amazing," he said with a smile.

"What?"

He wrapped an arm around my shoulders and tugged me close, kissing the top of my head. "You're every bit as smart as you are beautiful."

I flushed with pleasure, trying to hold back a grin. It was no use. The grin escaped, along with an embarrassed little laugh.

My insides were warm and mushy from the compliment.

I was a goner.

"Well, let's wait and see if I'm right before we sign me up to be a member of Mensa."

Caphy took off running. For a minute I panicked, thinking she was running after a coyote. But she headed straight for the door into the hangar and started digging at the threshold as she'd done before, whining.

"Something's in there," I told Hal in a hushed voice.

"Or someone," Hal agreed. He looked at me. "I don't suppose I can convince you to stay back?"

I blew a raspberry.

"Someone needs to protect LaLee," he tried, looking smug as he made the attempt. Clearly, he thought my softer side would help him win the argument.

I laughed, nodding toward the structure. "Too late."

The cat was sitting next to Caphy, licking a paw as if to say, "Hurry up minion, my manicure's getting ruined out here in the wild."

Hal sighed. "I'm surrounded by stubborn and impossibly reckless women."

Ignoring him, I headed over and tried the door. To my shock, it wouldn't open when I turned the knob. I looked at Hal. "It's locked."

"Did you lock it after the police were here?"

"No. In fact, I was down here the next day to clean up, and I'm sure I left it unlocked. I figured there was no point since Devon had been living here for weeks despite the locks on this door."

"Do you have a key?"

I thought about it for a minute. I had one at the house, but I really didn't want to trek all the way back. My dad had left a spare key somewhere...

It came to me a minute later. "The tank!"

I hurried over to the big, rusted fuel tank near the oversized hangar doors and bent down, skimming a hand over the thing's underbelly near the support leg. I felt the rough outline of the key after just a moment of fumbling around. "Got it!"

Tugging it free of the duct tape my father had used to keep it in place, I jogged back to Hal and handed it to him.

He inserted it into the lock.

It didn't work.

I gave Hal an incredulous look. "I can't flippin' believe it! He changed the lock."

I pounded on the door. "Dev, open the door and let us in."

We waited, listening to the silence. Caphy cocked her head a moment later and then started digging at the threshold again, whining.

LaLee seemed to grow bored with the show, wandering away and jumping up onto the sill of the office window.

Hal and I looked at her. Then we looked at each other. The cat just might be an alien from outer space after all.

Hal walked over and carefully scooped her off the sill. "Smart girl." She gave him a throaty yowl, clearly annoyed to have been removed from her high spot before she was ready.

I scratched her between the ears by way of an apology.

She hissed at me for my effort.

Hal pressed his fingers against the glass and tried pushing it up, likely hoping it was unlocked.

Of course, it wasn't. He glanced at me, lifting a midnight brow.

"Yeah, go ahead and break it. We need to talk to him."

Hal looked around for something to break the glass with and found a big rock. "Grab the cat," he instructed as he stepped away from the window.

I carefully scooped her up, offering a silent prayer to the goddess of cats that she wouldn't sink her pearly whites into me. She yowled with indignation, but let me hug her close. To my shock, she even purred a little. "Come here, Caphy girl." My dog trotted over to me, her ears pinched against her head with uncertainty when she saw who I was holding.

I tugged her several feet away as Hal lifted the rock and threw it at the glass. It shattered violently, but most of the glass followed the rock inside. He pulled his sleeve over his hand and knocked a bigger hole that he could reach through without slicing up his arm.

Unlocking the window, Hal tugged it open.

He peered carefully through, his gaze sliding around the room. "It's empty."

But something shifted inside. A figure leaped up from behind the desk and ran toward the door. Hal whipped around. "He's making a run for it. Is there a back way out?"

"Another door," I said, nodding.

He took off around the building. "Stay here in case he comes this way."

I frowned but realized that made sense. I walked over to the big hangar doors and tried them, settling the cat on the ground as Caphy trotted along beside me.

I heard footsteps pounding across the concrete floor inside. "Devon? Just come out here and talk to me." The footsteps stopped, but he didn't identify himself. Then inspiration struck. "We already found her," I told him. "You don't need to lie to me anymore."

A moment later the lock on the small door clicked, and a second lock snicked open. My eyes went wide as I realized he'd installed a deadbolt too. I hadn't even noticed the change.

The rat.

Devon came outside and stood staring at me with an angry glare on his bristled face. I was caught off guard, wondering what he could possibly be mad at me about. He was the one who'd apparently claimed squatter's rights to my dad's hangar.

But my heart softened when I saw how tired he looked. Purple arcs underscored his dark brown gaze. His face was thinner than I remembered, hardened from harsh circumstances and scored with deep lines where once round cheeks had been the predominant feature. His hair was more gray than brown but it was short, just touching the back of his neck, and looked clean. He also wasn't dressed like a homeless person any more. In fact, his clothes were respectable and looked clean. Though the big hands hanging down by his sides were calloused and work reddened.

I walked over to him. "I can't believe you didn't tell me."

He shrugged. "It was her wish. She was trying to keep you safe."

A soul-deep anger flashed through me. I was sick to death of people hurting me in the name of keeping me safe. "That's just stupid. If somebody wanted to harm me, they'd have done it by now."

Dev scratched his bearded chin. I was happy to see the bushy mustache was gone. "That's just wrong, Joey. They don't bother with you because they believe she's dead. If they find out she's alive, you become a very handy bargaining chip. She couldn't risk that."

"Bargaining chip for what? What does she know that someone would kill to protect?"

He shook his head. "It's not my place to tell."

I bit back frustration. I'd hit a brick wall. Two brick walls, actually. And I wasn't going to break through unless or until they decided to tell me what was going on. But there was one thing I could still find out. "What do you know about the murder of the real estate agent?"

His gaze skittered away. "I have no idea what you're talking about."

Hal rounded the far end of the long building at a run. "He ducked out the back. I lost him in the trees..." My PI skidded to a halt, his handsome face showing surprise.

"I've got him," I called out. But my rather obvious declaration did nothing to clear the surprise off Hal's face. He strode quickly toward us.

"He wasn't alone," Hal accused as he approached. "He's the distraction. His buddy hoofed it out the back."

Dev's face turned red. "That's a pretty nasty charge, Amity..."

"That might be," Hal responded, his hands clenching into fists. "But it's the truth, isn't it?"

As Devon bristled, his shoulders squaring, I realized I'd have to step in or they were going to come to blows. The two men had a rough history based on very different ideas of how to keep me safe. I lifted a hand, addressing myself to Hal. "Let's just calm down. Dev's going to come clean. Aren't you, Uncle Devon?" I asked.

I'd thought using the term of trust and affection I'd used for him all my life would soften him up a bit. Or at least shame him into cooperating. But I was disappointed as he vehemently shook his head.

"If there was someone else in that building, I didn't know it." Some of the color leached out of his face. "It might be one of *his* guys. If so, then we're all in danger."

His words were the distraction he'd probably intended. "Whose guys? Why are we in danger?" I asked, even as an icy band of dread gripped my lungs.

Hal stepped closer. "Medford's? You think Medford sent someone here to deal with you?"

Devon scowled at Hal's words and turned to me. "I'm not sure about the details yet, honey. But I'll find out. I promise."

Hal's head was shaking before Dev finished speaking. "Not good enough, Little. A real estate agent was killed on Joey's property. Strangely enough, here you are again. Just like you were the last time someone was murdered on this property."

"I told you I had nothing to do with that!" Devon yelled.

I placed a hand on his arm. He turned an angry expression to me. "Did you by any chance use the leash I had hanging on the hook by the office door?"

He frowned. "Leash? What leash?"

I opened my mouth to tell him and then decided just to go see for myself if it was still there. I turned away and went inside. The office door was fifteen feet down on the wall directly to the right of the entrance. It stood open. I glanced inside and was relieved to see that it was still relatively clean, as I'd left it. But there was a sleeping bag in the corner facing the door and a mug that still steamed with coffee on the desk. I glanced toward the coffee maker on the cabinet against the wall and noticed the pot was filled with coffee. Boxes of non-perishable items sat on the cabinet next to it.

Dev's clothing spilled from a duffle bag on the floor. Two shirts were hung over the chair and the lamp, clearly having been recently washed.

The series of small hooks hanging on the wall next to the office door were full of old hats, random keys and, on one hook, the old umbrella I remembered my father using when he had to walk home during the rain.

The thought spurred a memory which stabbed my heart like a blade, bringing fresh pain that made it hard to breathe. Finding out my mother was alive seemed to have reinforced the realization that my father wasn't.

And freshened the pain of his death.

"Is it there?" Hal asked.

I swung to face him. I'd been so lost in thought I hadn't heard him approach. "No." I glanced one last time to the hooks. The center hook where I'd always hung Caphy's spare leash was empty except for a grease-stained ball cap. "Not here."

"Why are you wondering about that leash?" Dev asked from where he lounged against the door frame.

If I didn't know what a great liar he was, the perplexed look on his face would have convinced me he was innocent. "The realtor was strangled with it."

His eyes went wide. "Then whoever did it..."

"Has been in this building," Hal finished for him, his dark gaze narrowing with accusation.

"It wasn't me," Dev insisted. "I'd have no reason to kill the woman."

"Who said it was a woman?" Hal snapped out.

Dev's gaze widened but he recovered quickly. "Aren't most Realtors women?"

My heart sank. "Oh, Dev."

"I didn't kill her!" my parents' oldest friend yelled. "You always assume the worst of me." He addressed the last to me, a pained, accusing look in his eyes. Then he spun on his heel and, before we realized what he was doing, disappeared out the door and slammed it closed behind him.

Something smashed against the door as Hal ran after him, shaking the door in its frame. By the time Hal got his hand on the knob to release the door, it wouldn't open.

He slammed his big body against the door several times before it finally crashed open.

Unfortunately, by the time he'd broken through, Devon was gone.

CHAPTER SEVENTEEN

Frustrated by how my day had gone so far, I asked Hal if he wanted to stay for dinner, call for a pizza or something.

He scoffed at my pizza suggestion. My PI's body was a temple. He believed eating healthy made him sharper in his job. He was probably right. But pizza and pie were much more fun.

We ended up going into town to pick up the makings for a pasta primavera. Hal assured me it was his specialty.

He pulled into the parking lot for *Junior's Market* and parked. As I climbed out, I heard angry voices and turned to find the tall, slightly pudgy form of Junior Milliard bending threateningly close to a woman who seemed vaguely familiar.

"Isn't that Penney Sellers' partner?" Hal asked.

The memory of my conversation with the realtor dropped into place. "Madge Watson."

He nodded.

We stood near Hal's car and watched for a moment, interested in the body language between the two. Madge stood with her arms crossed under her breasts, her gaze lowered and her lips compressed. She didn't say much as

Junior seemed to berate her for something. But when he reached out and poked her shoulder with a sturdy finger, her head came up and fear transformed her mulish expression.

Hal was on the move before I could suggest we step in. "Mr. Milliard," Hal called out. "Can I speak to you for a moment?

Madge used his intervention to make her escape, hoofing it quickly toward a medium-sized white sedan.

I gave Hal and the grocer a last look, wishing I could be in two places at once but knowing Hal would fill me in on anything I missed. I hurried after the realtor. "Madge! Do you have a minute?"

She opened her car door and looked up, frowning. "I'm sorry. I'm in kind of a hurry..."

I picked up the pace. "It won't take long, I promise."

She swung her gaze back to Junior Milliard. I noted that the grocer was standing with his head lowered, his face flushed. He was probably getting a verbal beating from Hal for bullying a woman.

Good.

I stopped in a spot that would block Madge's view of the two men. "I just wanted to make sure you were okay," I told her in a gentle tone. "That looked pretty intense."

Her lips quivered and her eyes filled with tears she blinked away. "It's fine. Just a little disagreement about the price of beef."

I highly doubted that. "Are you sure?"

She nodded, sniffling. "Now, if you'll excuse me."

But I couldn't excuse her. Or at least I wouldn't. "I notice you don't have a grocery bag in your hand."

Her lips compressed into a tight line. "You should probably just mind your own business, Ms. Fulle."

"You're right. I probably should. But there's something

about having a woman die a violent death on my property that brings out the nosy in me."

She looked into the distance, her expression softening. "I'm sorry about that."

What a strange thing for her to say. "You have no need to apologize. You didn't kill her. Did you?"

She shook her head, swiping angrily at a tear that had escaped her iron control. "Kill her? No. Of course not. She was a difficult person, but Penney was my friend." Her gaze sharpened. "I didn't know her death has been ruled a murder. I thought she'd simply fallen into your pond and hit her head."

"The police said she didn't die from drowning. She was strangled."

Madge's pale blue eyes went wide. "Seriously?"

She looked genuinely surprised. "Unfortunately, yes. Have you thought of anybody who might have wanted her dead?"

"No." She rubbed her arms and shivered. "That's horrible. Do you think it was an angry client?" I realized she was afraid for herself. If the emotion was genuine, that certainly changed things.

"It's definitely possible. She's made a lot of people angry over the last weeks."

Her gaze slid to Junior again.

I had an idea and went with it. "Is that what you and Junior were fighting about? Had Penney ruffled his feathers? Maybe he was angry at you for defending her?"

She wouldn't meet my gaze. Finally, she sighed. "No. I wish that was all it was."

"Tell me, Madge. Maybe we can help."

"We?"

"Hal's a PI. He's helping Deputy Willager on this case."

Something I couldn't identify flashed through her gaze. It almost looked like fear. Whatever the emotion was, it passed quickly. She stuck a leg into her car. "I wish you luck with that. I liked Penney and I'd love to see her killer thrown into jail."

I watched helplessly as she slammed her car door and started the engine, pulling away and leaving without a backward glance.

"No luck?"

I turned as Hal joined me. "How can you tell?"

He chuckled. "You have that look on your face."

"What look?"

He wrapped an arm around my shoulders. "That look that says you're not going to stop digging until you dig up some people who are speaking Chinese."

I let him lead me back to the car. "We're not going shopping?"

"Not today."

I thought his change of mind was strange, but I had more important considerations at the moment. "Chinese! You're a genius."

He opened the car door for me. "Huh?"

"We'll have Chinese food for dinner. You can pick something appropriately healthy and tasteless and I can order something good."

"You're incorrigible. You know that?"

I pecked him on the cheek. "Nope. Just hungry. And..." I added with a grin. "A much better judge of good food than you are."

"I never realized a cat could beg," Hal said as he fed LaLee a bite of his shrimp. The cat took it from his fingers very daintily and licked her paws afterward as if she'd been clutching the treat herself.

The pibl was not licking her paws. But she was giving me the laser gaze as I ate my dinner. Like me, Caphy preferred the gastric delights of all things fried and heavily sauced. She lay on the couch next to me with her squishy head on my thigh, her eyes following every arc of my fork from plate to mouth.

I offered her a piece of orange chicken. She took it carefully from my fingers. "Tell me what you and Junior talked about." We'd already exhausted all angles of my conversation with Madge Watson. Madge was clearly not telling us everything she knew, but neither of us really believed she'd killed her partner. So that still left us searching for the culprit.

I gathered from what little he'd told me, that Hal had come up as empty as I had.

"Junior was evasive too." Hal said. "He claimed Madge and Penney had tried to shake him down to get him to sell the grocery."

"And a common theme rears its ugly head again," I murmured.

"Yeah. But when I pressed him, he said Madge denied knowing anything about Penney trying to buy *Junior's Market*. He even admitted she was convincing."

"Then why was he so angry?"

"I think it was because he'd just found out he was the victim of title theft. He was sure the two realtors had something to do with it. It's looking like Cal's theory might be spot on."

I was lifting another succulent chunk of orange chicken to my mouth but, at his words, my hand stopped in midair. "Someone stole the title to *Junior's Market?*"

"That's what he said." Hal frowned. "If that's the scheme, everyone Penney Sellers harassed in *Deer Hollow* is in danger."

"But I don't understand, why would she approach him about selling if she intended to rip him off for his title? From what I've heard, it's an online process. She would never need to step foot in the place. By harassing us in person, she brought herself into the limelight."

Hal shrugged. "According to what Cal dug up, there are different types of mortgage fraud. One scheme is to offer to help struggling homeowners refinance their homes for smaller payments. Then the thief purchases the home instead, using straw buyers, and pockets the money he borrowed for the sale and never makes any mortgage payments. The home owner loses the title to his home and the banks are out the money they loaned to the fake buyers."

"That's pure evil."

He nodded. "I'll bet if we asked the people on this list, some of them talked to Penney Sellers about the need to refinance. Even if they only mentioned it in passing."

I shrugged. "Scott Abels mentioned he was planning to refinance his home. He might have been on a short list for that type of fraud."

"He definitely could have been," Hal agreed.

I chewed for a moment. "Poor Junior. Do you think he can get his store back?"

"I told him to talk to Arno, but I don't know enough about this kind of theft to speak to it. The one good thing is, if Penney Sellers *did* steal the title to *Junior's*, she's dead so it's doubtful she'll take out any big loans on it or anything."

"Unless she had a partner," I said, thinking of Madge.

"Yeah. But either way, Junior's suspicion and anger make him our new prime suspect."

I didn't like that idea at all. Junior Milliard had already suffered a big loss. He didn't have a wife or kids. The store was his life. I'd hate to think he'd snapped and killed the realtor and was headed for prison.

But that certainly seemed the most likely scenario at the moment.

Silence descended on the room, broken only by the occasional impatient snort from my dog. Hal and I hadn't discussed the Devon thing since returning from the hangar. But we needed to talk it out.

Devon had the opportunity to kill the unpopular realtor, since he was squatting in the outbuilding. He had a plausible motive if he thought Penney Sellers was in danger of finding out something about my mother or if he thought she was threatening me in any way. And, despite what my mother said, he had the temperament. I'd seen how ruthless he could be to meet his own ends.

I wasn't going to be caught off guard with him again. "Do you think he did it?" I asked Hal.

He wiped his mouth with a paper napkin and placed it on top of his empty plate, settling it onto the table. "I don't know. Despite being angry and uncooperative, he just doesn't strike me as a murderer."

I blinked, confused. Hal didn't trust Devon Little, and he liked him even less. He felt Dev had abused my trust and put me into danger more than once. He wasn't wrong on either count.

Which was why I was surprised to hear him say he didn't think Dev had the temperament.

Then I realized I'd made a segue in my head and forgotten to cue Hal in. He'd been referring to Junior.

"What about Dev?" I asked carefully.

Hal's handsome face darkened in a frown. "He's definitely capable. He had access to the murder weapon. And he was apparently in the vicinity."

I nodded, knowing what we needed to do next. "Should I call Arno?"

His expression softened as he looked at me. But he shook his head. "I'll call him. I don't want you to be in the position of going against your mother and ratting out the rat."

Despite his harsh characterization of Devon, or maybe because of it, I smiled. "Thanks, Hal."

He stared at me for a beat, something that looked like regret sliding through his dark green gaze. Then he leaned forward and touched his lips to mine. The kiss was gentle and sweet, his warm lips tasting deliciously of seafood and a sweet ginger sauce. Then he broke the kiss and leaned back, pulling his phone from the pocket of his shirt, and dialed our resident cranky cop.

CHAPTER EIGHTEEN

Much to my relief, Arno came to us. He knocked on my front door a half hour later, and Caphy barreled toward the front of the house, barking. Her claws clicked rhythmically on the hard floor as she ran.

"Settle, Caphy girl," I corrected, waiting until she'd dropped to her haunches before opening the door. I kept a hand on her head to keep her from barreling into Arno and knocking him over. Not that he couldn't handle her weight. He was a big guy and she wasn't massive by any means, but if she caught him by surprise, she could easily take a full-sized man down to the ground in a very ungraceful manner. Only to sit on his chest and kiss him into oblivion once she had him down.

I'd seen that particular show more than once.

Arno accepted her smashing into his legs, curving into him as he scratched her side and ruffled her ears. Her tail hit the door with a whomp, whomp, whomp that sounded painful.

"Hey," I said to Arno.

He straightened and gave me a cool nod. "Joey."

Arno was almost always cool with me. As if he were perpetually ticked at something I'd done. It had only gotten worse since Hal had come into my life. I didn't know if that was because there had been two bodies on my property since then, or because I'd pushed my way into both investigations against the deputy's wishes.

Either way, I didn't expect my relationship with Arno to improve any time soon.

Caphy bounced past him and into the yard, heading toward the pond with ears flopping and tail perpetually wagging. "Come on in. Hal's in the kitchen."

Hal walked into the living room as I closed the door and offered the deputy his hand. "Arno. Thanks for coming over."

Arno shook my PI's hand, nodding. "I'm interested in hearing about this big secret you wouldn't talk to me about over the phone." There was definite censure in his voice. He directed it right at me.

I barely kept from sighing. "It's not a big secret. We just wanted to let you know Devon Little is back."

Arno stared at me for a long moment. Finally, he put his hands on his hips. "Back? Back where?"

"Right back where he was before, apparently," I said. "We caught him squatting in my father's old hangar again."

Arno swore softly. "Where is he now?"

"He ran from us. I lost him in the woods," Hal said firmly. He was trying to pull Arno's censure from me and fix it on himself. A selfless act of affection. I could definitely fall for a guy like that.

Oh yeah, I already had.

"That's just great." Arno scrubbed a hand over his chin. Despite Hal's attempts to shoulder the brunt of Arno's anger, the deputy threw me an accusing glare. "You didn't think to come to me *before* he ran?"

"It's not like we had hours to figure out what to do," I told him angrily. "We saw him, talked to him for a minute, and then he locked us inside and took off before we could stop him."

"Why is he back?"

I glanced at Hal, frowning slightly to let him know he needed to keep my mother's secret. He slid his gaze from mine, fixing it on Arno. "He still feels like he needs to protect Joey."

Not the whole truth, but definitely not a lie. "He's honoring a promise he made to my father. I think he's still spooked over the whole dead guy in the woods thing."

"If he's in overprotective mode, he has the perfect motive to kill a pushy realtor who's trying to talk you out of the home your parents built," Arno said.

I didn't like Arno's suggestion, but I couldn't deny it. "There's more. I kept an extra leash in the hangar, on a hook outside the office door. That's the leash the killer appears to have used."

Arno looked at his boots, a muscle in his square jaw flexing. "I'm not convinced Little didn't have something to do with the last murder, Joey. This just strengthens my suspicions."

"I know," I said softly. I'd stopped thinking about Devon Little as anything but a thorn in my side, but that didn't mean I wanted him to go to prison. "I just don't think he did this."

"You're not able to think rationally where this guy's concerned, Joey,"

Arno spoke gently to me, and his sudden kindness was almost my undoing. Tears burned my eyes. "That's not true."

But Arno wasn't deterred. "It's totally understandable. In your mind, he'll always be connected to your parents."

"It's not as black and white as you think, Arno," Hal said, dropping an arm around my shoulders in support.

"Then why don't you tell me the rest of the story? The part you're both working so hard to leave out."

My stomach twisted with alarm. Too late, I remembered it was a mistake to underestimate Arno Willager. He was a good cop, as sharp as they came, and he knew me pretty well. "I have no idea..."

"Save it, Joey," he growled out. He looked very pointedly at Hal.

I shook my head and Arno's gaze flashed back to me. "So, that's how it's going to be?"

"Arno..." Hal began.

But Arno held up a hand. "You're off the case, Amity." Arno's angry gaze found mine. "Both of you. If you aren't going to be straight with me, I have no use for you." He spun on his heel and headed toward the door.

I threw Hal a desperate look. He frowned and looked away. He didn't blame Arno and he didn't want to lie to him anymore. I understood. But I couldn't destroy my mother's trust.

Could I?

"Wait, Arno," I said.

He stopped with his hand on the door, not turning back. I stared at his back for a beat and then sighed. "My mother's alive."

I saw him tense, the knuckles on his big hand turning white. He slowly turned around, but his gaze skimmed past me, locking onto Hal's.

My PI nodded. "We spoke to her."

Arno seemed to deflate. He shook his head. "It's not possible. I saw her remains."

I swallowed hard. "You saw the body of a woman and assumed it was her. But it wasn't. It was someone my parents were trying to hide."

"Hide?" Arno moved closer, his face a few shades paler. "Who were they hiding, and why?"

I gave him a quick update, skimming as quickly as I could over the woman who'd made my mother cry.

"So, they were going to hide her here? In *Deer Hollow*?"

"Only for a short time," Hal offered. "According to Joline, they'd planned on helping her move on as soon as it was safe."

Arno chewed on that for a moment and then scrubbed a hand over his chin. "I feel like such a fool. I should have run DNA on the victims."

"There was no reason to," I said. But I knew it would have been prudent.

"Clearly, there was," he said angrily. "I should have known better."

"None of that matters now," Hal said. "The fact is, everything Devon Little has done up to this point has been to keep Joline and Joey safe. We have no real evidence against him."

"We'll see about that," Arno said. "I've sent the leash to the lab for DNA. If he used it to kill someone it will show on the leash."

All the blood rushed from my face. "My DNA will be on there too."

Arno nodded. "But I have Amity's statement that you were with him. You're in the clear on this, Joey."

I glanced at Hal, flushing as I remembered how *that* had ended. I shook my head. "I really don't think he did it."

"We'll let the facts speak for themselves."

Hal spoke up. "There's something else. There was someone in the hangar with Little when we found him. I saw him run away but lost him. Little denies knowing there was someone there, but I'm not sure I believe him."

"Any idea who it might have been?" Arno asked.

Hal shook his head. "Little speculated it could be the

person responsible for the plane crash. He's worried for Joey's safety."

Fixing me with a speculative look, Arno nodded. "If he's telling the truth, Joey could be a target. I don't think we should take any chances. Can you stay here with her, Amity?"

"Of course."

I shook my head. "That's not necessary. I have Caphy..."

"Which wouldn't be any use at all against a gun," Arno reminded me.

I winced. The last time Caphy had tried to protect me she'd gotten badly hurt. I never wanted to experience the terror of that again. "You're right."

"Where's your mother?" Arno asked me.

"She's in a safe place."

"I need to speak to her. If the people who killed your father are here, there's a good chance they killed Penney Sellers because she was nosing around in the wrong place."

"I promised..."

"You just got her back. Do you really want to risk losing her again, Joey?"

I chewed my lip, uncertain how to move on. He was right. If Medford's people were skulking around my home, they might have killed the agent. And it was only a matter of time before they found my mother. But I couldn't betray a promise. "I'm sorry, Arno."

"Dangit, Joey!"

Hal held up a hand. "How about a compromise?" When Hal got Arno's full attention, he offered his proposal. "Why don't I interview Joline about it? I'll come to you with everything I learn. You have my word."

Arno skimmed a glare from me to Hal and then reluctantly nodded. "I guess that will do. But if I find out you withheld any information, Amity..."

"I won't. I want this guy found as badly as you do, Arno. Trust me."

"I *am* going to trust you. Both of you. I just hope I don't regret it."

After Arno left, I looked at Hal. "There's one other person we need to talk to."

"Who's that?"

"Edward Johnston. I spoke to his wife, but he was absent when I was there. At least, she told me he was gone. I'm not sure I believed her."

"Why not?" Hal asked.

"I don't know. There's just something about their part in all this. Neither of them has an alibi, and Belle Johnston admitted she wasn't exactly upset that Penney Sellers got clocked over the head."

"Joey, they're almost eighty," Hal said. "Besides, wanting to clock that Realtor over the head seems to be a town-wide infection, not a unique perspective."

"I know. But they're hardly feeble. They take good care of themselves, and they still do all their own work around that big house and grounds. If nothing else, I'd like to mark them off the list."

He nodded. "We can do that. I also want to check into Junior Milliard."

"You don't really think he killed her, do you?"

"No. But, like the Johnstons, he needs to be checked off the list. Right now, he's a giant question mark in my brain."

"Okay. Do you need to go home to do your research?"

"Yes. And I don't want to leave you here alone, so you're coming with me."

I would have argued, but then I remembered the pie. If I was really lucky, that banana cream pie he'd gotten for me would still be in his refrigerator.

What? A girl needed energy to catch a killer.

CHAPTER NINETEEN

Hal's background check on Junior turned up a whole lot of nothing. The man had led a boring, with a capital B, life. He didn't have so much as a parking ticket attached to his name. I shoved the last bite of pie in my mouth and licked my lips. "I guess he's clean, huh?"

"He has a clean record, but I'd feel better if he had an alibi. Even the most rule-following choir boy can snap under the right circumstances."

"I'd say losing his whole life in the form of *Junior's Market* would probably do the trick."

Hal nodded. "Exactly."

"What about Edward Johnston?" Though my stomach was already sticking out from the enormous slice of banana cream pie I'd eaten, my gaze was drawn to the last piece in the foil plate on the counter.

"Touch that and you die," Hal murmured. He never even looked up from the keyboard, where his long, blunt-tipped fingers danced so rapidly I could barely follow them.

"How do you do that?"

"Hmm?" he asked.

"Know what I'm thinking even before I do?"

His grin made my stomach turn a little gooey. "I'm an investigator. I'm good at investigating. In this case, there wasn't much to investigate. You. Pie. Trouble."

I couldn't help returning his grin. "I shared half of this slice with Caphy."

"Half?" He questioned with a lift of one dark eyebrow. "You gave her one tiny bite. It's a good thing you don't crave her kibble like you do that pie. She'd be skin and bones."

"That's a lie!" I frowned but couldn't help wondering if it was true. If Caphy's diet required regular slices of banana cream pie, would I leave her hungry to appease my own cravings? I hoped not. But my mind and motives were not always perfect where pie was concerned.

LaLee jumped up onto the kitchen table to oversee Hal's work. He frowned at the sight of the cat sitting on his pristine table, but happied up when LaLee rubbed her face on his arm, purring loudly.

"Aw, look, she likes you."

"She's probably just softening me up for the kill," he murmured direly. But I saw the twinkle of pleasure in his sexy green gaze. I watched him type away for a few minutes. Caphy was draped over my feet, keeping them warm, and LaLee was sprawled across the table, her gaze locked on Hal's dancing fingers.

A line appeared between his dark eyebrows.

"What is it?"

"I don't know, probably nothing." He turned the laptop so I could see the screen. It took me a moment to realize he was looking at the Johnston's bank statement. "You can do that?"

"Apparently I am," he grinned.

I leaned closer, narrowing my gaze at the columns of numbers. "Okay, what am I looking at?"

"See this here, and this, and this?" He pointed at some

fairly large deposits. They were irregular, no apparent pattern to their appearance on the screen. Some months he had one deposit. Other months it was several. The total in their banking account was sizeable. Much larger than I would have expected to see, given the way they lived. But whatever the deposits represented, they weren't enough to cause alarm compared to their overall amount. "Social Security checks?"

He shook his head. "They're close to the same amount but enough different that I doubt its either retirement or social security."

"Do they all come from the same place?" I asked.

He nodded. "That's what's really strange. The deposits are coming from Handy Loans."

I frowned. "Handy Loans? Isn't that a paycheck funds advance place?"

"It is. The question is, why would Edward Johnston be getting advances on money at all? He's obviously got a sizeable amount of ready cash in his account."

"That is strange." I glanced at Hal. "Shall we go ask?"

He nodded. "We shall."

∽

As I approached the big, rustic ranch house again, I hoped Edward Johnston was at home. There was a bright yellow, two-door sports car in the driveway, and I could hear piano music through the door as Hal knocked. Belle had been a piano teacher once upon a time. I couldn't help wondering if the car in the drive meant she still was.

Hal whistled, running his hand over the car's curves. "Nice ride. Somebody's got a healthy bank account. My gaze slid to the mud-covered Jeep parked next to it. "And somebody likes to go off-roading." I wondered which of the cars belonged to Belle and which belonged to Edward.

The front door opened, and a tall slender man with intense gray eyes and an unruly cap of charcoal-gray hair looked out at us. For a moment I thought he struggled to remember who I was. Then Edward Johnston smiled, transforming his face from slightly intimidating to handsome. "Joey Fulle." He reached out and enfolded me in a warm hug. He smelled like fresh air and pine sap. That, and the fact he was dressed in loose-fitting jeans and a flannel shirt, made me think he'd been working outside again.

"Hello, Mr. Johnston. How are you?"

"I'm just swell, little lady." He stepped back and eyed me from head to toe. "My goodness, you've certainly grown into a pretty little thing. The spitting image of your mom." His smile wavered slightly, and he clasped one of my hands between his. The skin of his hands was warm and slightly calloused. Edward Johnston was obviously a man who liked to use his hands. "I don't think we've seen you since your parents were killed. I'm so sorry for your loss."

I fought to control my expression, not wanting him to see my happiness and misunderstand it. It would be a relief when I could tell everyone my mom was alive. "Thank you. That's very kind."

He glanced at Hal. I hurried to introduce them. "Mr. Johnston, this is my friend, Hal. He's helping Deputy Willager find out who killed Penney Sellers."

The elderly man shook Hal's hand. "I don't envy you that task, son. I'm certain the list of suspects is very long."

"It's a pleasure to meet you, sir."

"Oh my goodness. Belle's going to string me up. Where are my manners? Come in. Come in." He stepped back and we entered the house. I glanced toward the stilted-sounding music and Belle waved at me. A small girl with stringy brown hair sat on the bench next to her, plucking away at the keys with the tip of her tongue sticking out. The child's mother sat in a chair nearby. As I looked her way, the woman's head came up. She smiled when she recognized me, waving.

It was my friend Sally Winthrop, the nurse from the hospital. She waved me over, and I excused myself, leaving Hal to follow Edward into another room. From where I stood, it looked like a library of some kind, with dark green walls and built-in bookshelves painted bright white.

I slipped into a chair next to Sally. "I didn't know you had a daughter?" I really needed to keep up with my old school friends better.

Her eyes went wide. "Oh, no, she's not mine. My cousin got called in for an extra shift. I'm off until this evening, so I offered to bring her for her lesson."

I vaguely remembered Sally's cousin, Pam. She'd been a couple of years ahead of us in school. "How is Pam? I haven't seen her in ages."

"She's good. Busy. You know, three kids in four years and a pretty intense job."

"Is she a nurse too?"

"Forensic Pathologist. She works in Nashville."

"In the Medical Examiner's office?" Sally nodded, wincing at a particularly unfortunate key choice across the room. She leaned across the small, round table between our chairs. "I hate to break it to her, but this one's not going to be touring the world with the *New York Philharmonic* any time soon."

We shared a grin.

"I remember when I insisted on taking ballet lessons at age five. My mom kept trying to talk me out of it, but I wouldn't bend." I shuddered. "I've seen the video. It was horrific. Like watching an elephant dance the waltz."

Sally laughed loudly, slapping her hand over her mouth when Belle glared her way. She mouthed "Sorry."

"It was the violin for me. I hit notes nobody's even

invented yet with that thing. I'm pretty sure I scared all the feral cats away from our house that summer."

I gave her a sympathetic wince. "So, did Pam get the leash for my realtor's murder?"

Sally shrugged. "No idea. She won't talk to me about her job. She works with the police in small towns all around *Nashville, Indiana. Crocker, New Fredrickstown, Deer Hollow.* But she's the most likely person."

We fell silent. I was wondering how I could ask her to try to find out the DNA result on Caphy's leash for me.

Sally winced again at the "music" staining the air around us, suddenly turning to me. "Oh, did you hear about Junior Milliard?"

I nodded. "I'm sure he's devastated about losing the store."

"I'd say he's devastated. That's usually what suicide means."

I blinked. "Wait? What?"

"Oh, sorry. I thought you'd heard, or I wouldn't have been so abrupt. Yeah, he was rushed into the hospital this afternoon. He took an overdose of pills. Poor guy."

"Will he be all right?"

"Physically, yeah. Fortunately, a customer found him in time. But mentally..." She sighed. "What kind of monster would steal someone's livelihood? It's evil."

I couldn't agree more. Then her words sank in. "Wait, you said a customer found him?"

"Yeah." Sally shook her head. "He tried to kill himself right in the pharmacy aisle of *Junior's Market*. He's just lucky he forgot to lock the front door. Otherwise, that real estate lady might not have found him in time."

My pulse shot into the stratosphere. "Real estate lady?"

"Yeah, Madge somebody." Her eyes went wide. "Wait, isn't

she the dead lady's partner? What are the chances of that?" Sally shook her head at the irony of it all.

"Yeah, that's quite a coincidence," I muttered. Trouble was, I didn't believe in coincidences that big.

I was dying to tell Hal what I'd learned. But I let him give me the low-down on Edward first. "Mr. Johnston does financial planning consultations on the side," Hal told me as soon as we were back in his car. "He says they don't really need the money. They've got a good retirement saved, but he likes the work. It makes him feel useful."

"I'm guessing that's the same reason Belle still teaches piano."

"Probably. Judging by the quality of her student's output, it isn't for the joy of the music."

I chuckled. "You should have been in the same room with it."

"I'll bet."

"Did he tell you why he was getting paid through Handy Loans?"

"Apparently, the firm that's hiring him out owns the place. It's just an easy way to move the money around."

I thought about that. It seemed strange. "A good way to hide the transactions from the IRS maybe?"

"I'm going to dig a little deeper into that. I'll call Pru and have her look into Mr. Johnston and Handy Loans."

To my credit, I didn't wince or roll my eyes. Prudence Frect was Hal's friend at the FBI. She was just as her name implied—perfect. She was tall, agile, beautiful and smart.

I hated her guts.

"Who was that woman you were speaking to?" Hal asked, interrupting my jealous thoughts. "She looked familiar."

"Sally Winthrop. And I'm sure you saw her in the hospital when you were attacked by the killer cat."

"Ah, you're right. I remember now. She wasn't one of my nurses, but I couldn't have missed the argument."

I lifted my brows. "Argument?"

"Yeah, she was having a fight with a dark-haired woman in a lab coat about something. I couldn't hear what the argument was about, but the other woman was really mad."

"She seemed fine when I saw her in the waiting room. It was probably just a disagreement about patient care."

"Probably. They were hugging by the time I left so they must have worked it out."

I nodded. "I learned something interesting from Sally."

"What's that?"

"Junior Milliard's in the hospital."

Hal's shocked gaze swung to mine. "How? Why?"

"Attempted suicide. Pills, apparently."

Hal paled. "I should have seen that coming." He hit the steering wheel with his hand. "He was so upset."

"It's not your fault, Hal. Junior was mad when we saw him. Not depressed. Besides, I'm not so sure it *was* a suicide attempt." He pulled into my driveway and stopped the car, turning to me expectantly.

I didn't make him wait. "You'll never guess who found him and called 9-1-1?"

"Our favorite real estate agent?"

I frowned, kind of disappointed that he'd guessed. "Well, dang."

Hal put the car into reverse and headed back out onto *Goat's Hollow Road*. I didn't ask him where we were headed. I had a pretty good idea I already knew.

~

Unfortunately, best-laid plans and all... Madge wasn't in the office and the building was dark and locked up for the night. Hal put a call in to Arno asking for Madge's address, but the deputy didn't answer. He left a message and pulled out of the *Deer Hollow Realtors* lot.

"Where to now?" I asked.

"To speak to J..."

He never got to finish the sentence.

I saw a blur of movement to my right and, before I could turn my head to look at it, the world exploded into a chaos of grinding metal, sparks, flying glass, and pain. The last thing I remembered before everything went dark, was getting punched hard in the face, and the sound of squealing tires as the freight train that hit us made its getaway.

CHAPTER TWENTY

Beeping.

Constant, annoying beeping. And disembodied voices filled with concern.

Those were the two things that greeted me as I slowly climbed back to consciousness. By the antiseptic stench and the constant movement that made real rest impossible, I knew I was in the hospital.

One voice in particular caught my attention and held, the deep, worried tones yanking me from unconsciousness like a slap to the face.

I tried to open my eyes, but they felt like they were weighted down.

A warm hand fell to my shoulder and gave it a squeeze. "Hey," Hal said. "How do you feel?"

I swallowed the lump of cotton clogging my throat and managed to drag one eye open, then the other. The room spun a little and my stomach quaked. For a beat, I thought I was going to hurl. "Like I've been hit by a truck."

"Well, you have. Or, at the very least, a big car. It's all kind of a blur."

I slowly turned my head. Even my neck hurt. Hal was sitting in a chair beside my bed, his dark gaze filled with worry. His face was swollen on one side, dried blood cutting across the scar on his temple and creating tracks leading to his chin. "You're okay?" I asked him. "You look like *you* should be in a hospital bed."

"I'm just a little dinged up. Your side took the worst of it."

A throbbing soreness had me touching my nose, and I flinched. "Ouch. Who punched me?"

"That would be the airbag, I'm afraid. You got a one-two punch because of the angle of the attack."

I thought about that for a minute, my mind still muzzy. Then his words clicked. "Attack?"

"Yeah, this wasn't an accident. If my car hadn't been so big and sturdy, we'd have probably both been killed."

"But who...?" I let the question trail away, my mind not up to the task of completing it.

"I don't know. Somebody appears to be cleaning house. I promise I'm going to find out."

I closed my eyes, lying back on the pillow, and felt drowsiness pulling at me. "So tired..."

"They gave you pain meds. Rest. I'll be right here."

I nodded and, licking painfully dry lips, let myself fall into the dark, velvet-lined tunnel that beckoned me.

When I woke up again, it was pitch black beyond the glass of the room's only window. I was lying on my side, my back to the door. A large man sat in the chair where I'd last seen Hal. But it wasn't him.

"Hey," the large man said.

I pushed against the unforgiving mattress and groaned as my bones and muscles objected to the movement.

Arno jumped up and reached out, gently helping me shift on the bed. When I was flat again, I glanced toward the door. "Hal?"

"He's just grabbing some coffee. Can I get you anything?"

I shook my head. "No. But thanks. Have you caught the guy who hit us?"

"Not yet. Hal's description of the vehicle is...unexceptional. I was hoping you'd gotten a better look."

"No. All I can tell you is that it was dark and boxy."

"Boxy like a van?"

"Maybe."

He nodded. "That might help." He sat staring at me for a long moment, his brown gaze filled with speculation.

"What?"

Arno glanced away. His big hands fidgeted on his legs. I noticed he was dressed in jeans and a tee shirt instead of the brown and tan deputy's uniform I was used to.

"Tell me, Arno."

"It's Madge Watson."

The way he said it told me all I needed to know. I swallowed another ball of cotton before managing to ask, "Is she dead?"

"Too close for comfort. She's in a coma. The doc thinks she's likely."

"Likely?"

"To die."

"Oh. That's bad, Arno. Her partner, Junior, now Madge."

"Yeah, I agree with Hal that somebody's cleaning house. Madge was found in her garden, her hand wrapped around the root of an aconitum plant. Highly toxic. Her gardening gloves were lying on the floor of her greenhouse. If she'd been wearing them, she'd have been fine."

I frowned. "I've never heard of a flower called Aco...whatever."

"Aconitum. You'd know it better as Monkshood. Beautiful but deadly. The root is the deadliest part of the plant. All she had to do was handle it and then rub her eyes or touch her lips."

"It sounds like she was a serious gardener," I pointed out. "She should have known better."

"Exactly. This has a professional stink all over it, Joey." He stared at me so intensely I knew he was telling me something important. But my brain couldn't quite grasp what it was.

Then it clicked.

"Garland Medford."

He nodded. "That would be my guess, yes."

"And if he thinks he's getting close to finding her?"

"He'll keep killing until he does."

My stomach roiled again, but it had nothing to do with the pain clenching my muscles. "You need to protect her, Arno."

"I would, Joey, if I knew where she was."

He held my gaze for a long moment. I had a decision to make, and it was the hardest one I'd probably ever make. If I sent Arno to my mother, I risked leading someone else to her too. I risked her life.

But if I didn't send him, I was also risking her life.

What would my father want me to do? That was an easy one. My father never trusted others to do what we could do ourselves. He'd have sent Dev...

My gaze shot to Arno's. "Devon."

"No sign of him."

"He's protecting my mom. I need to trust that he can keep her safe. He's done it for two years."

Arno sighed. He looked hurt.

"It's not that I don't trust you, Arno."

He stood up. "Except that you *don't* trust me, Joey. You've made that abundantly clear."

"No." I tried to sit up and fell back with a gasp as agony swept through me. I reached a hand in his direction, willing him to stay and listen to what I had to say. "I do trust you. But every person who knows is a potential weak spot. Devon's been able to keep her safe doing it his way for all these months. I want to trust him to keep doing just that. I trust *you* to find this jerk and take him down."

The door behind Arno opened, and a nurse came in. She held a clipboard in her hands and wore a surgical mask. She nodded at Arno.

He turned away. "I'll see you later."

I watched him go and sighed. He didn't understand my reluctance to let him in. I didn't blame him. But I felt like I was doing the right thing.

"How are you feeling?" The nurse asked, her voice muffled behind the mask. She stood a few feet away, checking the information on the clipboard.

"Sore," I told her.

"We can take care of that," she responded. Her eyes smiled at me over the mask. "You're due for pain meds anyway."

I glanced at the IV line running into the back of my hand. "Is this really necessary?"

"It was. I'm sure we'll be removing it later today."

There was a knock on the door and it opened. A man's head poked through. I wasn't sure if I knew him since he was wearing a mask like the nurse. The nurse slipped out of the room after murmuring something about coming back later.

The man I assumed was my doctor walked over and smiled down at me, his deep-set brown eyes crinkling at the corners. "I'm Doctor Lee. I've been assigned your case. How are you feeling, Ms. Fulle?"

"Fine." I was getting tired of answering that question. "Can I go home?"

"We'll see how you're doing in a few hours. You have a mild concussion. We want to keep an eye on that for a while."

I pointed to the mask. "Am I contagious? Everyone seems to be wearing those."

He chuckled. "No. Sorry. But we do have a rather virulent flu going through *Deer Hollow* right now. It's just a precaution."

I nodded.

He patted my hand. "Well, I'll be back to check on you in a few hours. You get some rest, okay?"

I nodded again, suddenly too drained to talk.

Doctor Lee nodded at someone in the hall as he stepped out of the room. A beat later, Hal came through the door carrying two Styrofoam cups. By the steam rising from the cups' contents and the smell wafting ahead of him, I figured it was coffee. The smell made my stomach protest.

He offered me one of the cups. I shook my head. "Thanks, but I don't think I could keep it down right now."

"Nauseous?"

"A little."

He sat down on the chair next to the bed. "Doc told me you have a concussion and some bruised ribs."

I gave him a tired grin. "So much for HIPPA."

"Don't blame him. I told him I was your fiancé."

My stomach leaped at his words. It was all I could do to keep my expression neutral. I looked everywhere but at Hal.

"Arno's got men out trying to find the driver who hit us."

"I know. He was just here."

Hal nodded, grimacing. He had a pretty good goose egg on his forehead. "How about you? How are you feeling?"

"I've got a bit of a headache, but that's all. I'll be fine." He glanced toward the door, which the nurse had helpfully closed behind her when she left. "I just went over to see Junior."

I widened my eyes in surprise. "He's awake?"

"Barely. And he doesn't remember anything except being totally despondent about losing the store."

"So, he *did* try to kill himself?"

Hal shrugged. "Your guess is as good as mine. He didn't leave a note, and he can't tell me for sure."

"Does he remember Madge showing up?"

"No. He was already unconscious when she got there."

I thought about that for a minute, the effort making my head hurt. I rubbed my temple, frowning. "Arno told me about Madge."

"Yeah." He sighed. "This is just too many accidents for my taste. Somebody's clearly covering his tracks."

I plucked at a string on the thin blanket covering me. "He thinks it's tied to my mother."

Hal didn't look surprised.

"But you'd already figured that out, hadn't you?"

He sipped his coffee before answering. "I'd considered it, yes. These hits aren't being done by an amateur. Somebody's taking precautions to make them look accidental. This is a professional. I've got Pru looking at Medford's organization. If there's any link at all to what's going on here, she'll find it."

I thought about that for a moment. I glanced up, catching his concerned green gaze. "My mom believes Medford has someone here in *Deer Hollow*."

He nodded.

"If that's true..."

"It's someone who's lived here for a while. If it were someone new, your parents would have suspected him right away."

I nodded. "I hate the thought, but I keep coming back to it."

Hal finished his coffee and stood. "If you're okay, I'd like to go do some legwork."

"Sure."

He reached out and grasped my hand, then leaned over and gave me a gentle kiss on the lips. The sweet touch was like anesthetic, wiping away all sensation of pain as my brain focused on the pleasure. As he straightened I grabbed his hand. "Will you check on Caphy and LaLee?"

"Of course. That was actually at the top of my list."

Relief flashed through me, softening some of the tension from my muscles. I hadn't realized I'd been worried about them until that moment. "Thanks."

"My pleasure. I'm going to keep Caphy with me. I figure the cat is good at getting out of sight if it becomes necessary."

"I agree. And nobody would want to tangle with her anyway." We shared a smile, remembering how painful our mutual introduction to the Siamese cat had been. In that moment, I realized how attached I'd gotten to the crotchety feline in the short time I'd had her. The idea of rehoming her no longer gave me any pleasure.

"I thought I'd stop by the barn too."

He spoke softly, his statement tentative, like a request. With my mind caught up in thoughts of LaLee, his words didn't click at first. Then I realized what he was telling me. I was torn. I didn't want my mom to hear about the crash—and me being in the hospital—and assume the worst. But every visit to her hidey hole had the potential to lead danger to her doorstep. I'd asked Arno not to go. How could I agree to have Hal visit her?

"I'm not sure that's a good idea."

"I have a way that will be perfectly safe."

"Oh. How?"

"Trust me?"

Of course I did. "Completely."

He squeezed my hand. "Get some rest. You'll be dealing with a manically concerned pibl later today."

I started to laugh, until agony stabbed into my ribs like a blade. Then I lay back and prayed that nurse would return soon with my pain meds.

I tried to rest as I'd been instructed. I really did. But, apparently, my room was a big draw in the small hospital. It was probably only thirty minutes later when there was another knock on my door. I forced my eyelids open, wishing everyone would just leave me be.

An attractive woman in a lab coat stood in my doorway, smiling brightly at me. She wore her chin-length, dark brown hair in a pageboy, the bangs forming a straight line above her golden brown gaze. The woman stepped into the room as soon as she caught my gaze.

"Hi, Joey. I heard about your accident and just wanted to stop in and see how you were."

I struggled to put a name to the face, unsure how to respond since the woman seemed to know me, but I didn't recognize her.

She lowered herself into the chair beside my bed and tucked a lock of shiny brown hair behind one ear. "Sally told me she ran into you and that it was your property where that poor woman was found."

The fog cleared and the woman's features snapped into place in my memory banks. She was ten years older than the last time I'd seen her, and she used to bleach her hair blonde in high school, but I finally recognized her. It was Sally's cousin, Pam. "The real estate agent," I said. "She came to my place trying to buy it out from under me and I sent her away. She turned up dead a few hours later."

Pam wrinkled a pert nose. "That's really weird."

"Welcome to my life," I groused. I immediately regretted

my grumpiness, and gave her an apologetic smile. "Sorry. My head's killing me. I'm afraid I'm not very good company."

She lifted a hand. "No worries. I don't blame you. I get downright nasty when my head hurts." She looked around the room. "I spoke to Doctor Lee on my way in. He said you'd be going home today. That's something, right?"

I started to nod and stopped when my brain seemed to slam around in my head. Where the heck was that nurse with my pain meds? "I can't wait. I'm going to take about six Ibuprofen when I get home." I rubbed my temples, wincing.

Pam looked alarmed. "You'll talk to Doc Lee about that first, right?"

"Of course. I was just being melodramatic."

The tension went out of her slim shoulders. "Good. I can stop by the nurse's station on my way out if you'd like. Sometimes they get busy and schedules suffer."

"That would be great. Thanks, Pam."

She nodded and stood. "Well, I'll get out of your hair..."

"Before you go..."

She cocked her head, waiting.

"I was wondering what you found on that leash you tested. Any recognizable DNA?"

She sighed. "Other than yours?"

When I cringed she shook her head. "Don't worry. I'm pretty sure Arno doesn't suspect you. I did find a sample with a familial match."

"What does that mean?"

"It means someone you're related to used the leash at some point. A parent or a sibling." Then she narrowed her gaze at me. "But you don't have any siblings, do you?"

"Nope. Just me."

"Yeah, so I'm guessing your mom or dad used the leash in the past?"

I nodded. "It would have been a couple of years ago though. Would the DNA still be there?"

"If the leash was kept in a fairly protected spot, it sure could be."

"I kept it inside, hanging on a hook. It's actually been so long since I used it, I'd forgotten I had it."

"There ya go. So, other than your family's DNA, there was nothing I can match. But I did find a tiny sample that we can use to prove the killer gripped it once we know who that is."

I really wished real life was more like TV, where they always knew exactly who the killer was from the DNA. Unfortunately, even I knew that wasn't real life. "Whoever it is doesn't have DNA on file?"

She seemed to be considering whether to answer my question, which told me she'd found a match. "It's okay. Hal and I have been helping Arno with the case."

She bit her lip and then nodded. "Actually, the DNA was in the database. But it was from a cold case in Indianapolis. The police haven't found the killer yet."

Ice crawled up my spine. We had a known killer in *Deer Hollow*. That put a whole new spin on things. Hal and Arno had been right to speculate that the killings were professional.

Then my mind skimmed to Devon. I wondered if they had any DNA on file for him. I couldn't bring myself to ask, not wanting to be the one to point a finger in his direction. I thought about the people we'd spoken to over the last couple of days and another name popped into my mind. An admitted sociopath. "Do you do psychological evaluations in your job, Pam?"

"Occasionally. I don't have a lot of training in that area, but I did minor in Psych in college and have taken some behavioral psych training. Why do you ask?"

"Do you know George Shulz?"

She gave the usual grimace when his name was mentioned. "Unfortunately. I needed a lawyer to help me with some private legal stuff a while back."

"Do you think he's a sociopath?"

She barked out a laugh. "He's definitely a horse's behind. And he certainly has some of the markers of a sociopath. But he seems to really like those cats." She wrinkled her nose again.

"Not a fan of cats?"

"No, I am. I love cats. In fact, I've been considering getting another one since my old tabby died last spring. But he doesn't clean up after them, and that office is disgusting."

"I can't disagree with that." It occurred to me that Pam would be the perfect person to take LaLee. But I was reluctant to bring it up.

"Why do you ask?"

Something in her tone of voice told me she was more than curious about my answer. She seemed surprised, almost suspicious that I'd singled him out. I shrugged. "He helped my friend Hal buy Devon Little's cabin. We went to speak to him about Devon, and he acted very strangely. I just wondered if he might know something."

I knew it was weak. I couldn't clue her in on the connection between Devon and my mother or the possible connection between my mother and the killer. So, I gave her the only thing I had. "He told us he was a sociopath. I found that strange."

"Yep. That is strange. I agree. But I have to say, Shulz takes great pride in being a cold-hearted jerk. I think he throws the sociopath label around to excuse his behavior. I wouldn't put too much stock in it."

"That's pretty much what Hal said too."

She nodded. "You're related to Devon Little, right? He's your uncle or something?"

I could see her scientific mind spinning with possibilities and was pretty sure she was wondering if he could have provided the second sample of DNA on the leash. "Not by blood, no. He was my dad's best friend, as well as my godfather."

"Ah." She still seemed more interested in Devon than she should have. "He was a suspect in another murder, wasn't he? Something about a painting?"

I sighed inwardly. I'd put her on Devon's track without meaning to. "The police believed he might be. He was eventually cleared." Sort of.

"Oh. Okay. Well..." She started for the door. "Take care of yourself. I'll see if I can get someone in here with meds for you."

"That would be greatly appreciated. Thanks, Pam."

"My pleasure."

I lay back and closed my eyes, willing my mind to rest. But Pam's information, along with my own speculation about George Shulz, had my thoughts spinning. Could Shulz really have killed Penney and attacked Madge and Junior? And if so, then why? What was the connection between them all?

Then it hit me. There was only one connection that I knew of, and it was a strong one. Schulz was a lawyer. The only lawyer in *Deer Hollow*. Which all but ensured that everyone in town would bump up against him professionally at some point.

As I realized that, I also realized Shulz would be a perfect plant for Garland Medford. He was well known and in a position to interact with almost everyone. Also, there was no danger he'd form attachments that would interfere with his spying. By his own admission, he was a cold, unfeeling man. He'd be the perfect spy for someone who wanted to find a woman with too many connections in the area to leave it behind.

And Uncle Dev had used his services to sell his cabin.

My eyes popped open. Of course! I was an idiot. There was the second connection between Shulz and the realtors. Hal admitted dealing with Penney Sellers over the cabin. *Deer Hollow Realtors* had listed it!

I opened my eyes just as the door swung open and a nurse I'd never seen before came inside. She said hello, her voice husky and muffled behind the mask I was no longer surprised to see.

I glanced around and tried to sit up. "Do you know what they did with my personal stuff?" I asked her. "I need my cell phone."

She shook her head, pulling a syringe out of her pocket. "Your stuff's in the closet. But you can't use your cell in here. It interferes with the equipment."

"I bit back a frustrated response. "Okay. Any word when I'll be going home?"

She shook her head. "I was told you need some pain meds?"

"Yes, please! Everything hurts."

"I'll be glad to help fix that." She moved closer and injected the contents of the syringe into my IV. Then she smiled, her eyes glittering hard and cold over the mask. "There ya go. In just a few minutes, you won't feel anything at all."

CHAPTER TWENTY-ONE

In a horrified flash, I recognized the voice. For a moment I was confused. Her presence there, and the coldness of her behavior, didn't match up to my expectations. Then, like a movie on fast forward, all the pieces clambered through my brain, falling over one another to shove themselves into a single, coherent picture. I knew suddenly who the killer was. Just as I knew I was about to die.

I cringed back, bumping up against the side rail on the other side of the bed. "I can't believe it..." I murmured, my hands fisting in the sheet as I tried to come up with a way out of my current predicament.

I had no Caphy to save me.

No Hal...

The "nurse" moved quietly to the door, turning the lock. "This won't hold for long if somebody gets pushy. But I'm pretty sure nobody's going to come, and you're much too weak to make much of a ruckus."

She was right. My limbs were getting heavier by the second.

"Your very cute private investigator isn't coming to your rescue. By the time he returns you'll be long gone."

No! I tried to move, but my legs were like lead.

She tugged the pillow from under my head. Horror razored through me as I realized what she was going to do. "He won't believe this was natural causes. Hal will find you. And you'll spend a really long time in prison."

She shrugged. "I'd do that anyway, wouldn't I? After killing your father and that meddlesome agent." The cold gaze glittered with malice or humor, I wasn't sure which. Maybe both. She didn't seem in the least bothered by what she was about to do.

"Pity you didn't die in the crash. You've been so difficult. Just like your parents." She sighed. "I should have known your mother would survive. She's like a cockroach, that one. A very lovely cockroach." Something wistful slid through the icy gaze above the mask.

Desperation filled me with frost. She fully intended to kill me, and I was helpless. I couldn't move so much as a finger to stop her. I had to keep her talking and pray someone came to help. "You don't want to do this. There's no evidence to prove what you've done. It's unlikely the police suspect you right now. I certainly didn't. But if you kill me you'll bring more heat down on your head." As I said the words I knew they were true. I'd considered just about everybody else. But not her. "If there was any evidence against you, Arno would have already made the arrest."

She laughed and the sound was bitter. "It's only a matter of time though, isn't it? You and that PI just dig and dig and stick your noses in where they don't belong. You were going to find me out. Best I clean up before that happens."

She moved closer, lifting the pillow over my head.

My mind screamed to strike out, get away. But my body wasn't cooperating. "Why?" I was shocked by the screeching tenor of my voice and regretted it when her gaze turned to ice. "Why are you killing all these people? I deserve to know that, at least."

"No. You deserve nothing. But I'm a fair person, so I'll tell you. Your parents crossed the wrong man. They never should have helped that scheming witch escape with his money. She left a trail of devastation behind. The rest of us have been paying the price for it ever since."

"Money? I'm sure my parents didn't know she was carrying around stolen money. They never would have helped her if they had."

She laughed, shaking her head. "So naïve. Your parents would steal a homeless man's last moldy bagel if they thought it would benefit them. I think you're old enough to stop believing in fairy tales, Joey."

I would have shaken my head in denial, but the drug she'd given me was disorienting me, and sapping energy from my body. I was so tired. So weak. I couldn't put up much of a struggle as she lowered the pillow over my face and pressed down hard.

Panic, rage, and fear warred for predominance as I strained against the immobilizing drug, unable to move or fight my fate. I struggled to breathe against the smothering softness of the pillow. And when I finally accepted that I would die, I prayed it would happen fast. That I'd pass out soon so the terror could end.

But, even as my lungs screamed for air, my mind gave me blurry, slow-motion reproductions of my favorite memories.

Playing hide and seek in the woods behind our house with my parents when I was five.

Dev and I creating a stage by hanging sheets from a tree and acting out a very bad Macbeth together for my parents when I was eleven.

Holding a tiny, quivering Caphy in my arms, and laughing with joy because my mother was going to let me keep her.

My tears soaked the cotton pillowcase as I thought of Caphy. I'd miss my sweet girl.

Hal would keep her for me. I knew he would.

Hal... So many opportunities lost. Love just beyond reach. It was tragic. But we'd experienced so much in the short time we'd been together. We'd become a couple.

I knew he and my dog would mourn me. Just as I'd mourned my parents...

Mother!

I wanted to rail and scream and pound my fists into the hateful creature ripping me from the world of the living.

I'd just found my mother again, and I was going to lose her.

It was so unfair.

Finally, I lost my awareness of everything beyond that clogging terror, my entire world wrapped around a single, terrifying sensation.

The agony of suffocation.

Then, miraculously, the pillow lifted. Not much. But enough for me to get a whisper of air.

I played dead, hoping she'd leave. But she wasn't paying attention to me.

She was half-turned toward the door as something thumped against it. There was another bang and it crashed open, slamming up against the wall behind it.

A banshee yell accompanied the lean, shrieking form of a woman, who propelled herself across the room so quickly my attacker barely had time to react.

The banshee threw herself at the woman with the pillow and they both crashed to the ground, shoving my bed sideways as one of them banged into it with a grunt.

I was so busy pulling wonderful, life-giving air into my lungs I didn't even notice Hal striding into the room at first.

But I couldn't have ignored my dog if I tried. Caphy leaped onto the bed and covered my face with kisses. So many kisses, in fact, that she was in danger of suffocating me all over again.

A big hand reached out and tugged her off my face, but left her on the bed with me, snuggled up against my side and whining pitifully.

"Are you all right?" Hal asked. He bent over me, pushing hair away from my face.

I managed a weak nod but my eyes kept trying to close.

"We need a doctor, stat!" Hal yelled.

A big woman who had carrot-colored hair and wore a pair of cotton scrubs flew into the room. "You can't bring that animal in here!"

"Hush, girl! The dog's staying. Go get the doctor as Mr. Amity said. And make it fast."

At the sound of my mother's voice, my eyes came open again. I watched her unfold herself from the floor as the nurse skedaddled back out into the hallway. She shoved golden hair off her face and looked my way, a beatific smile breaking out on her face. "Joey." Tears slid down my mother's face as she saw me. "I was terrified we wouldn't get here in time."

So was I!

My mom wrapped her arms around me and I finally relaxed, crying tears of pure happiness.

Doctor Lee came into the room. I was vaguely aware of him and Hal having a conversation, before I let my mind wander back to the woman crooning soothing nonsense words into my ear as she cried silently along with me.

My dog climbed onto my belly and closed her eyes, sighing happily now that she had me trapped beneath her.

Hal yanked my attacker off the floor and dragged her, none too gently, out of the room.

Doctor Lee yelled for a nurse and, a moment later, a male nurse was injecting something into my IV. Strength started to return to my limbs a few minutes later, and I was finally able to wrap my arms around my dog and my mom.

I was speechless with happiness. I'd gotten my life back. And I'd gained a mother. Life was nearly perfect.

I only wished so many other people hadn't had to die or suffer for my happiness.

Hal hovered over me, pestering me with questions about how I felt and if I needed anything. It became overwhelming, but I knew he was hovering for more than one reason.

Edward Johnston was in the wind. Belle must have warned him that we were getting too close. Or maybe it was Pru's investigation into his background and Handy Loan.

Pru had called that morning, the day after I returned home from the hospital, to report to Hal that Edward Johnston's little visits into Indianapolis had been all too suspiciously timed to the deaths of Garland Medford's enemies. Ten in all. And the payouts from Handy Loans happened just two days after each murder.

Handy Loans' ownership was buried under so many layers that Pru had almost given up before finally uncovering the name of the original owner, Larice Medford, Garland's long-dead mother.

Also, a search of the Johnston's home verified it was Edward's DNA that Pam had isolated on Caphy's leash.

The connection was clear. Edward Johnston killed people for pay. The sixty-five-year-old man was a contract killer. Pru had informed us he was over a decade younger than he'd led everyone to believe, probably to further the idea he was just a harmless old man. It was genius really. Even I hadn't seriously believed Edward and Belle were responsible for all the attacks because of their age.

Once Belle Johnston was in custody, Arno and two techs from the Indianapolis electronics division found an offshore account in the Cayman Islands that held a few million more dollars.

From all the signs, the Johnstons had been whacking people for a very long time.

I was still amazed at that. I'd known the Johnstons all my life. And, like Devon Little, they'd carried around secrets that seemed too incredible to be real.

I was a terrible judge of character. I said as much to Hal as he handed me a steaming cup of tea. He shook his head, lifting my legs and sliding under them before tucking the blanket firmly around my calves again.

"They fooled everybody, Joey. Not just you."

I knew he was right. But still... "Has my mom called?"

"Not yet. But she promised she'd check in as soon as she and Devon reached their destination. Wherever that was."

After finally getting my mom back, I'd had to say goodbye to her again. Garland Medford had lawyered up and disavowed any connection to the Johnstons' beyond paying them for legitimate financial counseling.

Pru and the FBI were working feverishly to find a connection they could use to bring Garland down, but to that point, they hadn't found so much as an email to use against him. Since the girlfriend who'd allegedly stolen from him had been misidentified in the plane crash, nobody even considered he might have been responsible for her death. And whoever my father's friend was who asked him to spirit the woman away, he or she wasn't coming forward with any information.

So, my mother had to stay in hiding for a while longer. I

hated it. But at least I knew she was alive. And I knew I would see her again in the future.

"How are you feeling?" Hal asked me for the hundredth time since bringing me home.

I sighed. "Why don't you go home for a while? I'm sure you have things to do, and I need..." I bit off my words before I told him I needed to be alone. "...to rest. I'm just going to take a nap with Caphy."

Hearing me use her name, Caphy's head popped up from the rug where she was sprawled not too far from the couch. She jumped up and bounced over, leaping onto the couch and stretching out alongside me as I scooted over.

Hal shook his head. "I could go get something to make for dinner tonight."

"Good idea." I thought of Junior. "Is the store open?"

"Yeah. Junior's back. And his memory's returning too. He remembers talking to Edward Johnston back by the pharmacy. About suppositories..."

Hal winced. And I laughed. "Seriously? That guy was really good at acting old and feeble."

Hal nodded. "Junior says he turned away to pull a box off the shelf and something slammed into his head. He doesn't remember anything after that."

"Edward hit him over the head like he did Penney Sellers."

"Yeah. And Madge too, it turns out. Which reminds me, I forgot to tell you, your friend Sally called this morning while you were in the shower. Madge came out of her coma. It looks like she's going to be okay. They found her in time and got the poison out of her system before it did any real damage."

"Oh good. That's a relief. Has Arno figured out how they were involved? And Penney too?"

"We think Penney saw Edward at the hangar that day

when she was snooping around. He was probably looking for Devon."

My eyes went wide. "He was going to kill him?"

"Or threaten to in an attempt to find out where your mother was."

I frowned. "You see, that's the part I don't get. Why does this Garland guy want my mother? His girlfriend's dead. My parents didn't have anything to do with her stealing his money."

"I don't think it was Garland who wanted her dead. I think it was the Johnstons. My guess is Edward Johnston reported to Garland that he'd killed your parents, but the girl escaped. He might have even accused Devon of helping her. Which would explain why Johnston was stalking him that day. He'd want to make sure Devon didn't talk either. If Garland knew the girlfriend was dead, he'd start wondering where the money ended up."

I shuddered violently at the thought of how close we'd been to coming face to face with a killer.

Hal patted my leg, giving me an understanding smile. "If I had to guess, Johnston got to the crash site that night before anybody else did, and took the money from the wreckage. If Garland finds out he has that money, he's dead."

"And he's worried my mother knows about the money and would talk if she was asked about it."

Hal nodded. "Exactly. Not to mention, if he believes she saw him at the site, he also thinks she can point a finger for their murder at him."

"But she didn't see him. I'm sure she would have told us. Or gone to the police."

"Probably, but it doesn't matter if she did or not. What matters is that Johnston believes she did."

"Okay, that all makes a twisted kind of sense. But why go after Madge and Junior? And why did Belle come after me?"

"Belle went after you because she was afraid you'd figure out that Edward had killed your father. But if you ask me, after listening to Arno's interview with her, I just think she hated your mother so much she wanted to cause her pain. There would be no better way than killing you."

"Plus, it would have drawn my mom out."

"It *did* draw her out. When Sally told us Belle Johnston was in the room with you, we panicked, and your mother took off. I could barely keep up with her."

"I can't believe she came out of hiding."

"When she heard what happened, I couldn't stop her."

"By the way, how'd you get to her place without being seen?"

"Through the woods on the 4-wheeler. Caphy enjoyed the run." He smiled.

"I'll bet. What about the others? Why did the Johnstons attack them?"

"Arno's talking to Madge now. She's got some short-term amnesia, but she remembers Penney calling her that day, telling her she ran into Edward Johnston at your place and that she tried again to get him to sell. Penney apparently had a soft spot for high-end homes, which was why she was particularly aggressive with you and the Johnstons. When Edward figured out that she'd told Madge, he was worried he'd be implicated in her murder."

"And I'm guessing he was right. Madge told Junior about Penney seeing him there because she wondered if Edward could have had anything to do with Penney's death."

"Yep. And since she and Junior were having a fling..."

I'd already put that part of it together. I nodded. "The day I walked into the realtor's office to speak to Madge, she'd obviously been busy with somebody. I heard whoever it was sneak out the back. And after seeing them arguing that day at *Junior's Market*..."

Hal nodded. "Junior believed Penny, and by association Madge, had been playing him for a fool to steal his store."

"But why would he think that?"

"Because Penney had been going around checking out all the homes and businesses in town, asking a lot of questions about them as if she were trying to assess their worth. It does no good for a thief to steal a title for a property that can't be borrowed against."

"And, as realtors, they'd be in a perfect position to deter-mine the value of properties," I added. "Makes sense."

"There's no indication Madge was involved in the theft. The journal you found seems to suggest Penney Sellers was involved in title fraud. I wouldn't be surprised to find out she'd been working with someone else though."

"My money's on George Shulz," I said.

Hal looked surprised. "Why?"

"Because I don't like him. And because I'm pretty sure he took money from Edward to tell him where my Uncle Devon was staying."

"You could be right. It would explain how Johnston knew to look at that outbuilding on your property."

I nodded.

A rusty yowl sounded from the floor, and I looked down. LaLee jumped up by Hal and rubbed herself along his thigh before climbing onto my belly and walking up to smear her face over my cheek. The happy rumble of her purring filled the room.

I didn't move for fear I'd scare her off.

Hal sneezed several times. "I forgot to take my allergy drugs this morning."

The cat jumped up onto the back of the couch and draped herself there, her eyes closing as she amped up the purring a few decibels.

"I keep expecting her affectionate rubs to turn into an attack," I whispered to Hal.

"Why are you whispering?" he asked me, grinning.

"I'm kind of afraid of what would happen if I startled her."

He shook his head. "Well, now that things have settled down, you can concentrate on rehoming her."

The cat's eyes shot open. She glared at him as if she understood.

I chewed my bottom lip.

Hal noticed. "You're thinking of keeping her, aren't you?"

I shrugged. "I'm really not..."

"Not what? Thinking about it, or keeping her?"

I stared at the purring cat, remembering Pam telling me that she'd like to get a new cat. Deep down, I knew Pam would give her a good home.

Still...

"Joey?"

My gaze slid to his and I saw humor lighting the dark green depths. A weight that had been sitting on my chest eased away. I gave him a slow smile. "I'm really not thinking about rehoming her because I guess I've already decided that Caphy needs a sister to keep her in line."

Hal barked out a laugh. Both animals glared at him for waking them up.

I laughed too. "You don't mind?"

"Of course not. It's your home and your decision."

"I know, but you're allergic, and I don't want to make you uncomfortable."

"If I take my meds I'm fine. In fact, she hasn't bothered me as much as I expected. And, strangely, she *has* kind of grown on me."

"I know, right?" I carefully reached up and scratched

LaLee between her pert, black ears. She stretched out her long legs and then hissed and smacked my hand.

Caphy's head came up and she barked.

LaLee hissed again and stood, stretching languidly before jumping off the back of the couch.

Moving slowly, cautiously, Caphy walked around the couch to see what LaLee was up to. A moment later the chase was on.

I wanted to bet on Caphy as they rounded the steps and headed for the kitchen. But the cat was hot on her heels, and I was pretty sure there was a nose scratch in my poor pitty's near future. Although, having seen them that morning, snuggling together in a warm ray of sun near the couch, I was just as certain my two fur babies would eventually become best friends. And my world would be all the richer for it.

The End

READ MORE COUNTRY COUSINS MYSTERIES

Did you enjoy **Mucky Bumpkin**? As my gift to you, enjoy Chapter One of **Humpty Bumpkin**, Book 1: Country Cousin Mysteries.

∽

She's just a country girl who loves her dog. But her life is about to get less countrified and more...erm...homicide.

Deer Hollow is a small community built in a verdant, rolling countryside. The nearest big city is over an hour away and big city ways are rejected at the Hollow. Unfortunately, the big city isn't the only place where bad things can happen.

Things like murder...which has a funny way of messin' up a debutante's day and turning a sunny Sunday in June right over onto its bucolic head.

Get **Humpty Bumpkin** at www.samcheever.com/books

HUMPTY BUMPKIN

CHAPTER ONE

The whole communication revolution thing is a mixed bag of wonderful and tedious. Things like cell phones are a revelation, allowing twenty-something women like me, who have trouble sitting still, to stay in touch with the important people in their lives while we go about our business.

But even the best innovations have their downside.

For example, a wise woman once told me never to answer a phone call whose number you don't recognize. *Answer at your own risk*, my cousin Felicity proclaimed one rainy day in the arboretum.

And I've since witnessed the intelligence of her advice. Several times over.

Unfortunately, I'm apparently a slow learner.

"Hello?"

"Is this Miss Joey Fulle?"

I frowned, not liking the "I want to sell you a bridge" tone of the caller's voice. "Nope, sorry. I think you have the wrong number."

"Actually, I believe I have the right number, Miss Fulle."

"You're not right," I said quickly and disconnected before the man on the other end of the phone had a chance to give me bad news. I had no idea what kind of bad news I was expecting. But I knew it was there, lurking like a vulture in a tree, ugly and ravenous.

I tugged the soft twisty off my shoulder length red-blonde hair and reached up to smooth the hair back into my favorite style, which was a high ponytail. Sweat dripped down between my shoulder blades and I was glad I'd dressed for the heat of an early June morning. Though my plain white tank top and cut off jean short shorts were already damp.

My dog, Cacophony, Caphy for short, bounded up and stopped in front of me, a clump of fur between her jaws. I grimaced. "Caphy, what did you do? Have you killed something again?"

A blonde pit bull with gorgeous green eyes, Caphy bounced several times, her muscular haunches springing her several inches off the ground each time, and then barked happily and ran off again, tail whipping the air. I sighed, knowing I should follow her and see if I could save whatever she'd decided to "play" with.

My phone rang again. I hit *Ignore* and trudged after my dog. "Caphy girl, where'd you go?"

The distant sound of barking drew me to a copse of old trees, their gnarled branches bigger around than I was and tangled together high overhead. It was behind one of these, an elegant old Elm tree whose knobby arms spread wider than the rest, that my dog was mostly hidden. I could see her butt wagging happily as she moved around behind the tree.

"Caphy, come!"

My sweet Pitty bounced out from behind the distant tree and grinned at me, her entire body vibrating with excitement.

"What have you found, girl?" I murmured to myself. "Come on, Caphy."

But she turned back to whatever she was exploring. That was when I realized she must have cornered something. I picked up the pace and hurried in her direction.

By the time I was fifteen feet away I smelled something rotting and knew that, whatever she'd found, I wouldn't be saving it.

Real panic set in. "Caphy, you come here right now!"

My dog disappeared behind the tree and I growled with frustration. But a moment later she reappeared, heading in my direction with something hanging out of her mouth. "Ugh!" I fought an impulse to turn and run. Being corpse-woman was not tops on my list of favorite things.

In fact, I was pretty sure it wasn't on the list at all. "Drop it, Cacophony."

Of course she ignored me, her steps becoming bouncier and more excited the closer she came. Clearly she wanted to share her treasure with me. I didn't know how to impress upon her that having a mangled, half dried corpse of a bunny or squirrel dropped on my shoes didn't take me to my happy place. My usual response of shrieking and running screaming away from her treasure just didn't seem to be doing much to teach her.

She was a very bull-headed pitty. I grinned at my pun.

Caphy ran up and dropped to her haunches a few feet away. She kept hold of the object, which I was trying hard not to look at, as if she was afraid I was going to take it away from her. She would be right about that. But it wasn't going to happen until I had a bag or something to use so I didn't have to touch it. I tried one more time to get her to let loose of whatever she was clutching between her jaws. "Drop it, girl." If I was really lucky I could convince her to let go of it and I could drag her home.

To my shock she lowered her head and released the contents of her mouth.

I glanced down. My stomach did a painful little dance and my gag reflex kicked in. Caphy was watching me very carefully, letting the object lie there as if checking to see how I would react. I was glad it was out of her mouth.

In fact, I would have been elated about it.

But I was too busy shrieking and running away. It might not work for her...but it worked just fine for me.

Deputy Arno Willager peered toward the object hulking under the trees. Two, skinny white stick-like things protruded from one end, their bony lengths painted in red streaks. He narrowed his dark brown gaze at the thing, no doubt gawking at the enormous feet on the end of the sticks.

I shuddered beside him, my dog vibrating excitedly next to me on a leash.

"Is this your chipper, Joey?"

I gave him the full force of my hostile blue gaze. "Uh, no, Deputy Willager. It's not my chipper. And, before you ask, that's not my body either."

He lifted a golden eyebrow and quirked wide lips as he skimmed my own personal body a long, slow look. "Oh, I can see that."

I frowned but didn't scold him for giving me the once over. I was on uneven ground with that one because I was pretty sure there'd been one time at a party in high school when I'd been in a closet with Arno, our star quarterback at the time. We'd been pretty drunk and the details of what we'd been doing in there were vague. I decided that changing the subject might be a good idea. "Do you know..." I swallowed hard. "—who it is?"

Arno wrinkled his nose. "Can't be more than a couple people around here with feet that big."

I nodded, covering my nose with a hand as a warm breeze carried the butcher shop stench in our direction. "It's horrible."

Arno didn't respond. Finally, I looked at him. "Did you call Doctor Miller?"

"I did."

"Well that's good." I glanced down at the item on the ground a few feet away. It was part of a hand. A man's hand if size was any indication. The ends of the fingers were missing, and my stomach roiled.

"Tell me how you found it."

"I told you already. "

"Humor me, Joey."

I sighed. "Caphy and I were taking a walk. It's a nice day."

He scoured me a look and I fought a grin. He was just too easy to annoy for his own good. "Caphy ran up ahead and came back with fur in her mouth."

"Fur?"

"Well...I thought it was fur. But clearly it wasn't." My gaze skimmed to the small patch of scalp resting in the dirt where Caphy had dropped it.

"Did you walk up to the chipper?"

"No."

"You didn't touch anything? Move the body parts...?"

"Ew! Of course not. Why would you even ask me that?"

"It's my job."

Frustration twanged my last nerve. Arno had always been a man of few words, but he had to know I had about a thousand questions. As if reading my mind, he turned to frown down at me. The sun dropped slowly behind him, forming a backdrop for his tall, lean frame, narrow hips and broad shoulders. Arno's face was classically handsome, with a clean-shaven square jaw, sexy brown eyes and a pleasantly-shaped mouth with a slightly fuller lower lip that was immensely appealing. Two lines rode the space between his dense golden brows as he looked at me. He was clearly chewing on something he thought he should tell me.

"What is it, Arno?"

The worry lines deepened and he held my gaze with a searching one. "You can't talk about this, Joey. This is an ongoing investigation and I need you to promise me you won't spill details around town."

"I don't know any details."

"You know more right now than anybody else except the killer." He lifted a golden brow for emphasis.

His words finally sank in. "Oh. Yikes."

"I need you to keep a low profile until we figure out what's going on."

"Surely this is someone from outside the *Hollow*."

He shrugged. "We don't know that yet."

I fell silent, chewing my bottom lip as a distant rumbling noise climbed ever closer to the spot where we stood. That would be Doctor Miller and the deputies Arno had called. They would have left their cars on the road and were approaching on all-terrain vehicles. My family's property included well over a hundred acres without roads. And the spot where Arno and I stood was in the most remote section of it all. The killer couldn't have found a more private spot to stick some poor schmoe into a wood chipper.

Finally, I nodded. "Okay. I promise."

"Good. Now you should get on home with that dog. She's disrupted the crime scene enough."

Caphy whined softly and dropped to her wide haunches, plying the deputy with a grin and soft eyes for good measure.

She wrung a grin out of him and he reached out to scratch the wide spot between her eyes. "You're a good girl, Caphy."

My pitty leapt to her feet and started wagging from her nose to the deadly whip of her tail, which unfortunately was smacking painfully against my leg.

I gave her leash a tug and, with one final look at the horror between the trees, we started back toward home. Despite my promise to keep the body in the chipper to myself, I had no intention of doing it. Whoever that poor soul was, he or she was killed on my property.

That made it personal.

And, personally, I didn't like it when people started flinging other people into wood chippers in my woods.

It was rude and disturbing.

And nipping it in the bud as quickly as possible seemed like the logical thing to do.

≈

Grab your copy of Humpty Bumpkin here: https://samcheever.com/books/humpty-bumpkin/

ALSO BY SAM CHEEVER

If you enjoyed **Mucky Bumpkin**, you might also enjoy these other fun mystery series by Sam. To find out more, visit the **BOOKS** page at www.samcheever.com:

Gainfully Employed Mysteries
Honeybun Heat Series
Silver Hills Cozy Mysteries
Country Cousin Mysteries
Yesterday's Paranormal Mysteries
Reluctant Familiar Paranormal Mysteries

ABOUT THE AUTHOR

USA Today and Wall Street Journal Bestselling Author Sam Cheever writes mystery and suspense, creating stories that draw you in and keep you eagerly turning pages. Known for writing great characters, snappy dialogue, and unique and exhilarating stories, Sam is the award-winning author of 80+ books.

To learn more about Sam and her work, visit her at one of her online hotspots:
www.samcheever.com
samcheever@samcheever.com

Printed in Poland
by Amazon Fulfillment
Poland Sp. z o.o., Wrocław